Maisey Yates

—

A Christmas Vow of Seduction

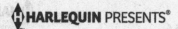
HARLEQUIN PRESENTS®

Recycling programs
for this product may
not exist in your area.

ISBN-13: 978-0-373-13860-9

A Christmas Vow of Seduction

First North American Publication 2015

Copyright © 2015 by Maisey Yates

This edition published by arrangement with Harlequin Books S.A.

For questions and comments about the quality of this book, please contact us at CustomerService@Harlequin.com.

Printed in U.S.A.

PROLOGUE

THE GIFTS HAD been on parade for the past hour. Shows of wealth from Tirimia being trotted out before King Kairos as though he were a boy and this was Christmas morning. Baskets overflowing with the finest fruits grown in the orchards from Petras's neighboring country. Art and jewelry from the most celebrated painters and silversmiths. But certainly the ambassadors from Tirimia had saved the most spectacular gift for last.

Kairos looked down from his position on the throne at the men who were standing before him, clearly awaiting his awe, and listened as they began to introduce their final treasure, the one they were calling the jewel of their collection.

"This will please you, my king," the man, known as Darius, was saying. "The ultimate in Tirimian beauty and grace, for your palace. For the continued health of relations between Tirimia and Petras. The representation of how far we've come since the revolution. It was bloody, and we cannot erase that history. We can only show we are committed to moving forward."

Darius was speaking of the overthrow of Tirimia's monarchy some fifteen years earlier.

Kairos had not been on the throne then, but his father had made sure he'd been well educated in what was happening. At the time, the rebels in Tirimia had even posed a threat to the borders of Petras. Earning back trust between the two nations had been slow. Which was why they had requested an audience with Kairos today. He was the newly installed king, and they were clearly keen to make the most of the clean slate they felt he might offer.

Too bad for them he wasn't easily impressed with baubles. However, they had quite a few natural resources he was interested in, and war was never in the best interest of the nation. Which was why he had granted them the audience. And watched with decreasing patience as they brought forth their offerings.

"As a token of goodwill between our nations," Darius said, a film of oil coating each word, "we present to you Princess Zara."

The doors to the throne room swung open and there, standing in the center of the doorway, flanked by two large men, was a woman. Her hands were clasped in front of her body, bright gold cuffs gleaming from her wrists.

For a moment Kairos wondered if she was bound. Then she began to walk, her hands falling to her sides, and that momentary fear was alleviated. Her hair was long and dark, caught back in a braid that swung with her every step. Her face was decorated with gold paint, dots above her eyebrows, and a few down below her eyes. She possessed a dark, exotic beauty that stoked no fire in him. She was so unlike his cool, blonde wife, Tabitha. The only woman he wanted. The woman who had chosen to skip this very important procession.

He wished, very much, that Tabitha were here to see this. To see him gifted with a woman. He wondered if her blue eyes would burn with jealousy. If they were capable of burning with anything at all.

Very likely, she would simply sit there, passive and unmoved. She might even suggest he take the girl as his own. So little was her esteem for him these days.

He ignored the kick of regret in his stomach.

"There must be some mistake," Kairos said. "I cannot imagine you intend to give me a human being."

Darius spread his hands wide. "We have no need of a princess in Tirimia. Not now."

"So you seek to give her to me?"

"To do with as you please. Preferably, you would take her as a wife. Her dishonor is not our wish. Though, however you intend to use her…it would be an honor in its way."

Another wife. He could think of nothing worse.

"I regret to inform you that I already have a wife," Kairos said, regretting nothing of the kind.

"If you do not believe in taking more than one woman in matrimony in this country, we would find it acceptable if you took her as a concubine."

"I have no positions available for a concubine either," he said, hardening his tone.

"We demand security," Darius said. "If we are to open up our borders to Petras, then we demand blood ties. This is the tried-and-true method of obtaining this level of security."

"And here I thought you were a nation moving into the modern era," Kairos said, looking down at the woman whose eyes burned with anger, who radiated energy, but kept silent, her dark head bowed low. "It seems to me that this stands in contradiction to that."

"Our system of government is young, while our country is old. The marriage between tradition and modern reality is, at best, a clumsy one. We must keep our people happy while moving into the future. Surely you can appreciate some of the issues inherent in that."

Kairos felt a smile curve his lips, an idea forming.

Andres. This would be the perfect occupation for him. A perfect bit of revenge that would satisfy the small, mean part of Kairos that had never fully let go of his brother's betrayal. It would also accomplish great things for the country. Vengeance that furthered his cause as ruler was a rare and glorious thing.

"As I said," Kairos spoke, surveying the room, "*I* already have a wife. My brother, however, is most certainly in need of one. She will be just perfect for him."

CHAPTER ONE

RETURNING TO THE palace in Petras was never Andres's favorite thing. He preferred his various penthouses scattered throughout the world. London, Paris, New York. And a beautiful woman to go in each one. He was a cliché, but he was comfortable with it. If only because it was so much fun.

Petras was never half as much fun. It was where his brother, Kairos, used an iron fist, not for the people of Petras, but for Andres himself. As though he were still a boy needing to be taken in hand, and not a man in his thirties.

Invariably, his stays in the palace followed a staid and steady routine. Visits to hospitals and other approved public appearances where his every word was carefully scripted. Stilted dinners with his older brother and his wife, which were as boring as they were uncomfortable; and long nights spent in his vast royal bedchamber *alone*, because Kairos didn't approve of Andres bringing lovers to stay in the hallowed halls of the Demetriou family. Though Andres thought that had less to do with propriety and more to do with the fact that Kairos was out to punish him for his past misdeeds in a million small ways, every day, until he died.

Which made his discovery, upon entering his bedroom, all the more remarkable.

He walked in tearing at his tie—too tight and constricting, like everything here—slamming the door behind him. Then he froze. There, in the center of his bed, knees curled up against her chest, long dark hair cascading loose over her shoulders like spilled ink, was a woman. They both regarded each other for a moment. Then she scrambled to her feet, stumbling backward on the mattress until her back was pressed against the large ornate headboard that had never been any use to him, as he'd never had a woman in *this* bed.

Until now.

Though she had not been invited, neither did she look very excited to be there. Both of those things were a bit of an anomaly.

"Who are you?" he asked. "What are you doing here?"

She tilted her head upward, her expression defiant. "I am Princess Zara Stoica of Tirimia."

Andres knew very well that Tirimia was no longer a monarchy. In fact, the royal family had been driven from the throne during a bloody revolution back when Andres was a teenager. He hadn't been aware there were any survivors, much less a princess who looked slightly more like a bedraggled creature than a woman.

Her bronzed skin was painted with gold, framing her dark eyes and eyebrows. Her lips were a deep shade of red designed to entice, but he had a feeling that allowing himself to be enticed could be a mistake. She looked much more likely to bite him than kiss him. Her hair hung down well past her backside, disheveled as though she'd been in a fight, or thoroughly pleased by a lover.

Because of the bed, it was tempting to imagine the latter. But judging by the expression on her face, it was most certainly the former.

"You seem to have the wrong palace, Princess."

"I do not," she said, her tone stiff. "I am a prisoner in my own country, and I was brought here as a gift to King Kairos."

Andres's eyebrows shot upward. His older brother wouldn't know what to do with a woman as a gift, even if he *weren't* bound by marriage vows. "In which case you're in the wrong room."

Her expression turned stormy. "He did not wish to keep me. He, in turn, gave me to his brother."

Andres could not process the absurdity of the statement. This woman, was a gift for him? "Are you telling me that you've been regifted?"

She frowned. "I suppose."

Clearly, she didn't see the humor in this. But

then, if he were the one being passed around like an unwanted present at a white elephant party, he might be humorless too.

"Would you possibly mind waiting here for a moment?" he asked.

Her expression turned stormier still. "I would not have been here at all if I had any other options. I have nothing to do but wait."

"Excellent." He turned on his heel and walked back out of the room, stalking down the hall, down the curved staircase that led to Kairos's office. He would no doubt find his brother bent over important paperwork, looking grave and serious and not at all like a man who had just given his younger brother a *woman* as a *gift*.

Andres pushed open the door to the office without knocking, and as he had guessed, Kairos was indeed sitting there laboring over work.

"Perhaps you would like to explain the woman in my bed?"

Kairos didn't look up. "Andres, if I were tasked with explaining every woman in your bed, I would never get anything else done."

"You know what I mean. There is a creature upstairs in my chamber."

Kairos looked up. "Oh, yes, Zara."

"Yes. A princess of some kind? She claims she's a prisoner."

"It's a bit more complicated than that," Kairos said.

"Enlighten me."

His brother actually smiled, the expression nearly knocking Andres to the floor. A smile on Kairos's face was a rare sight. "She was given to me by dignitaries from Tirimia."

"That much I gathered."

"As you know, I'm trying to reestablish trade with them. They are our closest neighbor, and being at odds with them is pointless. More than that, it can be dangerous and costly." Kairos's expression turned serious again. "Our father didn't see the point in mending bridges between the two nations. Here I sit, trying to restore Petras to its former glory, and this is one way I can accomplish that."

"By accepting a woman as a gift like she was an expensive watch?"

"Yes, Merry Christmas a few weeks early."

"Did you want me to keep her in my pocket and ask her the time?" Andres asked through clenched teeth.

"Don't be ridiculous. You're going to marry her."

Anger settled like lead in Andres's stomach. "Oh, I see. This is your belated revenge?"

"Again, don't be ridiculous. I've got a country to run. I hardly have time to seek revenge to the detriment of the people. Now, make no mistake, I may enjoy your discomfort a bit, but it is no less necessary that you make this union a reality."

"You have no reason to hold on to your anger where I'm concerned. You're better off with Tabitha than you were with Francesca anyway."

"That," Kairos said, "is debatable."

Andres had never been under the illusion that his brother and his wife were head over heels in love, particularly not given the circumstances surrounding the marriage. But this was the first time he had ever heard Kairos speak negatively about the state of things.

The fact that Tabitha, once his brother's PA, had turned out to be such a suitable queen was one reason Andres had been able to absolve himself of his indiscretion with Kairos's *first* fiancée five years ago in a Monte Carlo hotel suite.

He'd been so drunk that he hadn't remembered what had transpired between himself and Francesca. But there were numerous photos, and some very explicit video footage plastered all over the internet the following day that had left things in a very unambiguous light. Kairos had been forced to call off his marriage, disgraced and humiliated by his fiancée, and his own brother. Kairos hadn't loved Francesca, that much was clear, and his ire hadn't been born out of a broken heart, but out of the sting of public humiliation.

Shortly after, Kairos had announced his engagement to Tabitha, and the royal wedding had taken place as planned, on schedule, with a different bride. Everything neatly swept under the rug, as though it had never happened. Which made it easy for Andres himself to forget the part he had played in the way the dice had fallen.

But if things with Tabitha weren't all that they appeared…

"And what does that have to do with me?" Andres asked.

"I need you married. I need you to help with the relations between Tirimia and Petras. Princess Zara solves both of those issues. You need to grow up and start behaving yourself. I was lenient with you even after the stunt you pulled with my fiancée. I have been very patient until now. While you have continued to whore your way through Europe and the States, I took over the responsibility of running the country."

"So you're saddling me with a woman who seems to be here against her will?"

"You knew you would have to marry someday. This is no surprise to you."

"I figured I might have some involvement in the selection of my bride."

Kairos pounded his hand down hard on the desk. "Men like us never do. You have lived a life sheltered from the responsibility that faces us. I have not had that luxury. I know the reality of it. You marry appropriately. You do not marry for love. Yes, I suppose I should be thankful you spared me the scandal of having to divorce Francesca. But I selected Tabitha in haste and…it is entirely possible we are facing a larger problem than an issue of marital happiness."

"Are you unhappy?"

"I never expected to be happy. Neither do I require happiness." Kairos rubbed his temples. "What I require is an heir. It may have escaped your notice that I don't seem to possess one."

"I assumed you were trying for one."

Kairos curled his fingers into a fist. "We have never used birth control. Five years, and we have never tried to prevent pregnancy. Possibly more information than you would like, but now you know where things stand."

"What is it you are leading up to here, Kairos? I've never been accused of being the smart one. You have to spell things out."

"You may very well be responsible for producing the next in line to the throne. That means you need to marry. You need to marry royalty. Princess Zara is, in fact, royalty."

"You expect me to exit bachelorhood and start producing babies on such short notice?"

Kairos waved a hand. "Don't be so dramatic about it. Just because you marry doesn't mean you have to change your behavior entirely. Certainly you will have to be more discreet."

His brother suggesting something as shocking as carrying on extramarital affairs was surprising, and was almost as shocking as the fact that Kairos was essentially marrying him off. "Are you unfaithful to *your* wife?"

A muscle in Kairos's jaw jumped. "No. I'm simply telling you that things don't have to change all that much. Obviously your marriage will be one of convenience, and as long as you treat her with respect, I don't see why you should have to pledge your fidelity to her."

"I have no practice with fidelity. I would hardly stake my life on it."

"You knew the day would come when you would have to take some responsibility for the nation. That day is now. It's this. Father may have expected you to amount to nothing, but I certainly expect you to carry your weight."

"I had no idea that as the spare, I was required to carry any weight unless you died."

"Unhappily for you, that is not the case. I need you for political reasons, and practical reasons."

Andres looked down at his brother's dark, furious eyes. "If things are so terrible with Tabitha, why don't you divorce her and find a woman who can give you the children you need?"

Kairos laughed, a hollow, bitter sound. "There

are certainly some things you will have to learn if you're to be a husband. I can no more cast off my wife because she can't produce children than give a speech in front of foreign dignitaries without clothes on. I would be crucified by the press. I made vows to her, and I intend to keep them." He didn't sound happy about it, and certainly his devotion to her had nothing to do with love. That much was clear. "It's time to atone for your sins, little brother."

Andres was usually quite content in his sins, with no desire to atone for them at all. Except for Francesca. That he would take back a hundred times over if he could. Particularly now, with the stark reality of Kairos's marriage to Tabitha laid out in front of him, he could hardly defend those actions.

"You're overlooking a very important piece of the equation," Andres said.

"And that is?"

"She does not want to marry me. That much was clear when I encountered her in my bedroom. We're holding a kidnapped woman."

"She has very few alternatives," Kairos said. "I get the sense that if she goes back to Tirimia she'll be in danger. For all that their government is playing nicely with us now, things are far too tentative for me to stake her life on presumed decency. She is safest here."

"She's feral. What do you expect me to do with her?"

"You're a legendary playboy. The last thing you need from me is advice on how to deal with women."

"She is not a woman. She's a *creature*."

He thought of that wild dark hair, her glittering, angry eyes. Somehow they were supposed to make a royal couple? He would need a woman twice as tame as Tabitha to convince the public of a change in him.

A woman such as her wouldn't make his reinvention easy.

Kairos laughed, an even rarer occurrence than a smile. "I'm a married man, but even I noticed there was enough to recommend her. She's beautiful, though, I confess not overly sophisticated."

"I was too busy being surprised by her presence in my bedroom to notice her beauty." A lie. He was not blind to her curves, her full, sensual lips. Despite the fact that, for all he knew, she might attack him if he approached her, she was a lush little package.

"My word is law," Kairos said, his tone uncompromising. "And you owe me, brother. You will obey me on this. Tame her, train her, *seduce* her, I don't really care, but by God you will marry her."

Andres clenched his teeth together. He would find the moment more surreal if he hadn't long suspected that it was coming. That someday he would stand before his brother and be informed of his fate. He was a prince, the second born to an old royal family. He had never imagined he would escape marriage, children. It had always only been a matter of time. And his time, it seemed, was up.

"Anything else, Your Highness?" Andres asked, his tone dry.

"Don't take too long."

CHAPTER TWO

PRINCESS ZARA STOICA, heiress to no throne at all, was tired of waiting on the whims of men. It was because of men that she had been uprooted from the palace as a child, sent out to live in the deep, dark woods with the nomadic people who inhabited them, kept safe thanks to centuries-old traditions of honor and hospitality. It was men who had stolen her from her safe haven fifteen years later, and elected to use her as a pawn to further political unions with neighboring nations. Of course, it had also been a man sitting on the throne here in Petras who had decided it was perfectly acceptable to keep her and pawn her off on his brother as a sort of postwar bride.

As a result, it was not a terrible surprise that it was a man who clearly owned this room, and who had burst in close to an hour ago, nearly terrifying the life out of her.

It occurred to her that it was entirely possible she had been installed in Prince Andres's room. The man she was supposed to marry. The very idea made her shiver down to her bones.

Worse than fear was the restlessness starting to run through her veins. She was growing bored, closed up here in the bedroom.

There was a view of the city from a small window by the bed. She found no comfort in such a view. Houses clustered together tightly, high-rise buildings beyond that. Cars cluttering up the roads like a line of dizzy ants desperately seeking food. She preferred the crisp, clean air of the mountains. The silence held close around her by thick evergreens.

She had a difficult time marking passing hours while shut up in vast castles with nothing but man-made architecture sprawled out before her.

She flopped backward onto the bed, sinking deeply into the down-filled blankets and soft mattress.

It was shocking, being exposed to such comfort.

Her years spent living in caravans with her caregivers had been cozy, and not uncomfortable, but it had certainly been nothing like this. And when the new political leaders of Tirimia had brought her back to the old palace, they certainly hadn't installed her in anything half as luxurious.

She looked up at the ceiling, at the ornate molding, the large chandelier that hung from the center of the room. She could not recall ever having been in a bedchamber with a chandelier. Tirimia was a much more modest economy than Petras, even before the revolution.

A sense of unease washed over her and she

scrambled off of the bed. She did not want that man, whether or not he was Prince Andres, coming in and finding her like that again. It was unsettling. She paced the length of the room—and it was a fairly impressive length—before retracing her steps, pausing at a door that was firmly closed. She wrapped her fingers around the ornate knob and pushed it open, finding a vast bathroom on the other side. It was much more modern than the rest of the room.

There was a large shower in the corner of the room, glass panels closing it off from the rest of the space. There was also a large, sunken tub that nearly made her groan with longing. The very thought of submerging in warm water sent an intense craving through her that rivaled any she'd ever had for a dessert. A long, hot bath was something that was simply impossible out in the middle of the forest, and something that hadn't been afforded her when she was brought back to the palace as a glorified prisoner.

It was a temptation, but if she thought being discovered in a bed that was not her own was humiliating, certainly being discovered in the bath would be worse.

She walked slowly across the room, moving to a large vanity and mirror mounted at the back wall. There were small bottles displayed on the clean marble surface. She wondered what a man did with so many bottles of lotions and scents. She reached out and took hold of one, unscrewing the lid and lifting it to her nose, sniffing cautiously. It was a cologne, smelling of sandalwood and other spices. She tried to remember if the man she had encountered earlier smelled of those things. She could not.

She set the bottle back down, picking up the next one. This one contained lotion, and it was a temptation too far for her. She tipped it cautiously, squirting a small amount onto her hands, before putting the bottle back in its place. She smoothed the thick cream over her hands, luxuriating in the feel. Her skin had grown rough from so many years of hard labor and living outdoors. A sign of strength, she often thought, and she had never regretted it. Still, it didn't mean she couldn't indulge in one small moment of softness.

"What are you doing?"

She turned sharply, backing herself up against the edge of the vanity, knocking several of the bottles over as she did. "I was bored," she said, looking up to see the same man she had encountered earlier standing in the doorway glaring fiercely at her.

The impact of him was beyond that of a physical blow. She was accustomed to large men, men with a commanding presence that pushed you back, held you at a distance.

Some might call the people she had been raised with Gypsies, based on their simple, nomadic lifestyle, but they weren't, not in blood heritage. They were part of a small, mostly destroyed minority group in Tirimia who still clung to the old ways. Not a warrior culture in the traditional sense, but fiercely protective of the camp and of anyone they felt to be under their care.

However, the gruff exterior of the men she had been raised around could not have been more different from the suave, confronting aura given off by this man. One would think that a man in a suit would not be half as intimidating as one in old jeans. This man should have appeared to be vastly more civilized, and yet it was that veneer of civility that she found frightening. Because she sensed so much beneath it. A hidden depth and strength, buried so deep she had no way of assessing it.

She didn't like this at all. Didn't like the fact that she was in the dark about so many things. At home, things had been so much simpler. She had been protected. She had been certain of her surroundings. The world had been small, containing the forest, her caravan, the cooking fires and people she had known for most of her life.

There were rules. And she had been certain in them.

Now she was here. In a strange land, confronted by a stranger.

A large, broad-chested stranger in a well-cut suit. With short black hair, a square jaw and strong, dark eyebrows. He was beautiful in the same way a predator was. Lethal, and difficult to look away from. She had never, in all her life, been held captive by a man in such a way. So far the men she encountered could easily be divided into two categories. Those she had grown up with and seen nearly every day of her life, and those she considered an enemy.

This man was neither, and that made him unique.

She might yet decide he was an enemy, but for now, she would hold off on that assessment. He might well be dangerous, but he could also very well be her only ally. She had realized two months ago, when she was kidnapped from the encampment, that she had only a spare few options. If she tried to escape her captors and go back to the clan, they would be punished. A poor repayment for shared food, clothing and shelter of the past fifteen years.

Escaping and staying in Petras was no more of a possibility.

She had no money, no form of identification. She didn't know the layout of the city, or of the country beyond. She couldn't drive, and she had no friends.

She would have to make one.

Zara eyed the man standing in the doorway of the bathroom. She wondered if she could make a friend of him. Well, not a friend. Not in the true sense.

But it would do no good to battle him all the way. She would need to be compliant, to a degree. To watch for the right moment to make her move. Whatever it might be.

"You were bored?" he asked, repeating her words back to her.

"Yes, I don't know how long I've been in here, but it has been quite a while."

"Perhaps we should start over," he said. "I am Prince Andres. It appears we are to be married."

Unease, followed by a rash of unexplainable heat coursed through her veins. "Is that so?"

His words confirmed her suspicions. That he was the owner of this room. That he was now the owner of *her*.

"I am informed." He arched one dark eyebrow. "Perhaps you would like to continue this discussion in a more comfortable setting?"

She nodded slowly and began to walk toward him. Then her stomach growled, the sound echoing in the space. "I'm hungry," she said. She realized then that she hadn't eaten since very early this morning.

"Then I will arrange for you to be fed."

It didn't take long for Andres to procure the

promised food. He had a tray of meats, cheeses, fruits and breads sent up to the bedroom, which was how Zara found herself sitting on the bed again, her legs covered with a blanket, eating the spread that had been placed before her.

She could feel his watchful gaze on her as she ate in near silence. He hadn't interrupted her yet, but she could see that he wanted to. For the first time in a very long while she felt she might have the upper hand. A very *slight* upper hand, to be sure, but he seemed nearly as confused and put off by the entire situation as she was. Which was, in her estimation, why he was being so watchful. And why he was letting her eat undisturbed. He was circling her, as though she were a potentially dangerous creature and he was concerned about being bitten.

The thought sent a pleasurable rush of power through her, joining the sated sensation in the pit of her stomach brought about by the cheese. Her needs had always been simple. At least, they had become simple once she was sent to live with the nomads at just six years old. They had been simple by necessity. But lately, her needs had shrunk down even further. Warmth, food, shelter. If she had those things, she knew she could keep on going.

Good food and *soft* blankets were several notches more extravagant than she'd had in the past couple of months. And a bit of power? Very heady icing on top of this unexpected cake.

So she continued to eat in silence, sensing his growing impatience, allowing it to feed her small, mean satisfaction.

"How long has it been since you were fed?"

His question surprised her. "Since this morning."

"You are too skinny," he said, his tone matter-of-fact. His words offended her, and she couldn't quite figure out why. She had never given much thought to her appearance. The men who had taken her captive had assigned a woman to make her beautiful for presentation to the king, but Zara couldn't say it had mattered much to her. They had put too much makeup on her, the gold around her eyes her own addition, a nod to the culture she had adopted as her own. Her beauty had never been a topic of discussion among the nomads. She had been under the protection of the leader, Raz, and he had forbidden any man from touching her, or even looking at her in a disrespectful manner.

And now this man was telling her she was too skinny. And she was angry.

"I will say that my captors did not overly concern themselves with the quality of my food."

"You are a captive?" he asked, his tone fierce.

"I'm surprised you care. Your brother did not

appear to be similarly concerned. He was quick to accept me as though I were a…a fruit basket."

He looked her over. "You are most certainly not a fruit basket, that much is evident."

"I have been passed around like one." She sniffed, allowing herself a moment to fully revel in the indignity of it all. At one time, she had been a princess. A member of the royal family in Tirimia. Being in a palace such as this would have been her right. Before she had been wrenched away from the only home she'd ever known, robbed of her family. Her birthright. "I suppose I can only be grateful no one has plucked at any of my grapes and taken small samples, so to speak."

She looked up and caught his dark gaze, the sharp shock of heat piercing her straight to her stomach. She felt her face warm and she looked away. "Indeed, that would have been a shame. I'm glad your grapes remain…unsampled."

A muscle beneath her eye twitched. "Remarkable under the circumstances, I should think." She had spent a great many years being protected, but that did not mean she was ignorant of the ways of men.

"You were the princess in Tirimia," he said, his tone vaguely accusatory.

"I *am* the princess. I have been replaced. Not by another princess, but by a farcical government who pretends to care about the freedom of the people, when, in truth, they only care about their own power."

"I thought the entire royal family was killed during the revolution."

Her insides grew cold. That always happened when she thought of her parents. Of her older brother. Her memories of them were soft around the edges now, worn like old, weathered photographs. But what remained, as sharp and terrible as ever, was the coldness she'd felt when she learned of their fates.

It hadn't been sadness in its simplest form. It had been death itself. A chill that had stolen through her, replaced all of her blood with ice. It had taken months to thaw. Months for her to feel anything at all again beyond the frost that had taken up residence in her chest.

"Obviously I wasn't," she said, the words strange, thick on her tongue. Because they'd never felt right. None of it had ever seemed right. "Everyone else…my mother, father, my brother, they were all killed. My mother's personal maid had family living in the forest, people who practiced the old way of life. And she brought me to them. They have kept me, protected me, for years."

"Until now, clearly."

She picked up a piece of bread and tore a chunk from it. "Obviously not through any fault of their own. They were ambushed and I was kidnapped."

"And can you be returned to them?" he asked.

She weighed that question and all of the possible implications. If she told him yes, would he help her? Or was he intent on...marrying her.

The idea of marriage was ludicrous to her. Foreign. She was not in any way ready, or suited, to be a man's wife. She had no interest in such things.

The very idea was her worst nightmare. Wearing a crown again. Placed on a throne.

A target would be on her back, and she would be up on a pedestal where she was an easy target.

She had lived through that nightmare once. She had no intention of entering into it again.

She should tell him to take her home.

And have the only people on this earth who tried to protect you destroyed?

That bitter, familiar cold lashed at her again. She couldn't go back. It was too dangerous. It was selfish. They would protect her with their lives, and it was very likely their lives would, in fact, be the cost.

She had lost too much already. Too many people who had believed deeply in their convictions cut down. To hear Raz speak of her parents, her father had been a man of conviction. Who had fought to change antiquated ideas in Tirimia, who had made a pact with Raz's tribe to preserve their sovereignty within the nation.

For that, he had been killed. Out of loyalty and respect to her father, Raz had risked the tribe to protect her, to raise her.

She wouldn't put them at risk again.

This was something she would have to figure out on her own. She would have to rescue herself.

"No," she said. "I cannot be returned to them. It would be far too dangerous."

"Wonderful," he said, his tone at odds with the word.

"I will not be marrying you, of course," she said, taking a grape from the platter and holding it between her thumb and forefinger.

"Is that so?" he asked.

She nodded, keeping her expression grave. "I have no desire to marry."

"Why is that?" he asked, reaching out and plucking the grape from her fingers. "Concerned over having your grapes sampled?" He put the fruit in his mouth and she found herself transfixed, trying to untangle the wealth of meaning in his words while watching his lips, his jaw, work slightly as he chewed.

Why was the way he chewed interesting? It shouldn't be. She'd never found chewing fascinating in her life.

"I don't know you," she said, looking away and picking up another grape, biting into it with no small amount of fierceness. "And that's just for a start."

"We have nothing but time to work this out. You could list your reasons. Extensively."

"I won't have a complete list until I know you better."

"I think what you just described *is* marriage. Two people who truly don't know each other and are somewhat blind to each other's faults until time and proximity force them to really get a good look at the poor choice they made."

"You make it sound so appealing," she said, shifting her position, tucking her feet beneath herself and leaning forward, taking a piece of fig from the platter.

"I'm not a great believer in the institution."

"Then why should we marry?" she asked.

"Because," he said, his tone weary, "my brother has said it shall be, and so it shall be. There are a great many perks to being the spare in the royal family, Zara. Not the least of which is that I have been able to cast the mantle of responsibility off for the past thirty-two years with very few consequences. While Kairos has always been bound by duty, honor and all manner of other words that make me feel like I'm about to break out in hives. The downside," he added, leaning in, studying the platter, but not taking any more food, "is that I am also beneath his rule." Andres looked up then, his dark eyes meeting hers. He was close now. So very close.

And he did, in fact, smell like the cologne she had found in the bathroom.

"I see," she said, barely able to force the words out past her constricted throat. "Are you going to tell me you're a prisoner too?"

He straightened and she nearly sighed in relief. For some reason, having him so close to her was disturbing in ways she couldn't quite work out.

"No," he said, "I'm not a prisoner. Just a prince. That means there are certain expectations I'm obligated to fulfill. Make no mistake, I've spent the past decade and a half steeped in debauchery and generally ignoring all of my responsibilities. We all have to face a reckoning, eventually. You are mine."

Arrogant. That was what he was. To sit there and call her his reckoning when she'd been dragged here against her will. To speak of his duty as such a burden when her father had lost his life upholding the crown in Tirimia, fighting for what was right.

What did this man do with his position? Nothing, from the looks of things.

"You speak of being a prince with such disdain. I am a princess, forced into hiding because of the title. My parents were killed because they were royalty, and yet you stand here, perfectly whole, complaining of being forced into marriage by your brother. How terribly sorry I am for you that your life of extended pleasure is being interrupted by duty. My parents died for duty."

"Am I supposed to regret that that isn't an option for me? Should I go offer my neck to the guillotine rather than my hand in marriage?"

"My parents are dead," she hissed.

"And I am sorry. But I am not sorry that I don't face the same peril. This is not the same country, nor am I in the same position."

"You have your life and your opportunities and still you speak with such disrespect of the position."

"And still, you will be my wife."

"Never," she hissed, knowing that now, with hair tousled and her posture mirroring that of an angry cat, she was looking every inch the feral creature he clearly thought she was.

"What are your options, *agape*?" he asked, the endearment strange to her ears. "You said yourself you cannot return home. Where will you go if you don't stay here with me?"

Words churned through her mind, but when one would rise to the surface, it would slip back beneath just as quickly, before she could grab hold of it.

"Nowhere," he said, answering for her. "You can speak of life and death all you want, as though it is all that matters, but here in this position you see that. There are many shades of gray within living and death, and unhappiness through a forced marriage is most certainly one of them. But you're like me. You've hit a wall. You have no choice."

"There is always a choice," she said, not sure where the words came from, but certain, even as she spoke them, that they were true. "I live because of that truth. Because rather than giving up, my mother's maid chose to save me. Because rather than sending me back, the clan chose to care for me. We always have choices."

"I suppose you're right," he said, his dark gaze far too assessing. "Then this is my choice, and I'm making it. I owe my brother a debt, beyond the typical royal duty. I'm in no position to refuse his demands. And I choose to obey them."

"What of my choices?"

"They are somewhat crippled in this situation. I won't lie."

"Crippled? They are completely incapacitated."

He shrugged as though he were pushing her protests off his shoulders. "Perhaps. But this is the reality. Whether you want to or not, you, Princess Zara Stoica, will be my wife by Christmas."

CHAPTER THREE

"PRINCE ANDRES."

Andres looked up, at the servant who was standing in the doorway of his brother's study, the other man's expression concerned. Andres and Kairos had spent the evening playing cards and drinking Scotch. Possibly both avoiding the women in their lives.

Andres still had a hard time believing he *had* a woman in his life in any capacity other than his bed. In addition to the fact that she was his fiancée and not simply a lover, he did not want her in his bed. Not now.

He could no more imagine bedding that creature than he could imagine willingly sticking his hand into a badger den. Just another reason he'd tasked his brother's staff with placing her in a different wing of the palace.

He had spent the earlier part of the night discussing the marriage with Kairos. And Kairos's expectations. Of course, they would be figureheads for the nation. Actively involved in political and social events. A counterpart to himself and Tabitha, particularly important since it could potentially be up to them to produce heirs.

That meant they had to be at least half as respectable as Kairos and Tabitha, a feat Andres couldn't imagine either of them managing.

A concern only deepened by the very worried look on the servant's face. "Princess Zara refuses to be moved."

Andres dropped his cards onto the table in front of him. "What do you mean she *refuses*?"

The man cleared his throat. "She was quite… adamant. She says she is comfortable."

Kairos made a dismissive noise. "Unsurprising. She is already unwilling to leave your bed." Kairos sounded…envious. Kairos had it very, very wrong.

"That is not it," Andres said darkly.

Kairos raised an eyebrow, and Andres recognized his own features looking back at him. It was rare that he saw the similarities between himself and his brother, but he saw them now. "My wife quite happily has her own room."

"Mine most certainly will," Andres said, his voice a growl. "Perhaps a gilded cage is in order. One with a very firm lock." He sucked in a sharp breath. "I don't know how you expect me to make a princess of her."

"She is a princess," Kairos said, his tone bland.

"You know what I mean."

"I thought, perhaps, it might cost you so much energy to tame her that you might tame yourself in the process."

Andres glared at his brother, anger roaring through him. If only Kairos weren't so far from the truth. It was the very idea of managing to tame both of them that made it seem so impossible. He said nothing else. He stormed toward the door, and the servant stepped out of his way.

"If you cannot remove her," Andres tossed back as he walked down the hall, "I will do it myself."

He walked to the staircase, taking the marble steps two at a time before striding down the hall toward his chambers. He pushed the doors open and was met with an empty room.

His future bride was nowhere to be seen. He stalked through the room and approached the bathroom, flinging the doors open wide.

He heard a squeak, then a splash. He looked toward the bath where he saw a very wet, indignant woman.

"What are you doing in here?" she demanded, as though she were the royalty in the room.

He supposed, in all fairness, she was one part of the royalty in the room. However, the only thing she had ever ruled over was a campfire, if the information he had received on her background was correct.

"This, *Princess*," he said, his tone hard, "is *my* bathroom, in *my* bedroom. You were asked to move. It was brought to my attention that you refused."

"I am comfortable here," she said, sinking farther beneath the water, her expression stormy, her actions proving her words to be a lie. She was anything but comfortable, at least at the moment.

"What a terrible coincidence. I find that I am also comfortable here. As it is my room, with all of *my* things."

"I was brought here against my will," she said. "I am out of my element. I am frightened."

Anger fired through him. He wasn't sure why his reaction was so out of proportion with what was happening. It would cost him nothing to sleep in another room, and yet he found he couldn't let this go. Probably because Kairos was already maneuvering him as though he were a marionette. He had no choice but to allow that, as Kairos was the king here in Petras. However, he did not have to let this little *creature* maneuver him too. And he would not. If she was to marry him, then she would need to understand that he was not to be trifled with.

He had a reputation as a playboy in the media, as the more laid-back half of the two Demetriou brothers. But that only held as long as he went untested. As he was a prince, very few people had attempted to test him. But Zara seemed intent on doing so, and he could not allow it.

"I do not believe you are frightened," he said, moving nearer to the bathtub.

She lowered herself deeper beneath the surface of the water, until her chin was submerged, her large, dark eyes pinned on his. "Of course I am. You are very large. Much larger than I am. You have invaded my space."

"Begging your pardon, Princess," he said, moving closer to the bath, bracing his hands on the edge of the marble tile and leaning in. "It is you who have invaded my space. I did not invite you here. I did not get down on bended knee and propose to you, nor did I at any point surrender my own personal space to you for your continued use."

She squirmed, and he could see her crossing her legs beneath the water, raising her arms to cover her breasts as best she could. The details of her body were indistinguishable as it was, and her belated show of modesty only drew attention to that which she was trying to hide.

She was beautiful. He could not deny that. Acres of smooth golden skin, wide, dark eyes that were just as pronounced now with all her makeup washed off as they had been when they were rimmed with black and gold. Her lashes were long and thick, her lips full, her cheekbones high, giving her a proud, sensual look that would certainly turn heads wherever she went.

When it came to appearance, she was everything he might have wanted in a wife, in a princess. It was her manner that left much to be desired. In fact, her manner left everything to be desired.

He had not often thought of what sort of woman he might take as his wife, because he had put off thoughts of a wife, even though he knew he would someday take one. Still, in the back of his mind he had thought he would probably marry a woman who exuded a kind of serene sophistication. One who would make his life easier. The perfect accessory to all events. As necessary and yet understated as a nice pair of cuff links.

Zara was no more a cuff link than she was a fruit basket.

"I'm distressed," she said, her tone growing more arch by the second. "I was rooted out of my home only two months ago, held prisoner in the palace—"

"So I have heard. And while I do possess a small amount of sympathy for you, I am unsure what you expect me to do about it. You said yourself, I cannot return you to your family. You do not wish to marry me. You have told me that, as well. So here I have a short list of the things you cannot do, and the things you do not wish to do. If you could tell me one thing that you *do* want, that might be of greater use to me than hearing everything I am unable to do."

"I find myself quite comfortable in this room,

in this bath, at least I was until I acquired your company. With that in mind, perhaps you might let me stay here, as it is somewhat familiar."

"Are you so fragile that moving down the hall will disrupt your sensibilities?"

"I am quite fragile!"

He had a feeling that, had she been standing on dry ground, she would've stamped her foot to add punctuation to the statement.

"You are a great many things, but I would not characterize you as fragile."

"Leave me," she said, issuing orders like a queen.

"No," he said, "I think not."

He reached beneath the water, uncaring if the sleeves of his shirt were soaking wet. He wrapped one arm around her shoulders and the other beneath her knees, straightening, holding her naked and dripping wet against his chest. He did not look at her, keeping his eyes fixed straight ahead as he strode from the bathroom back into the bedroom.

"What are you doing?" She began to squirm, surprisingly strong, and difficult to maintain a hold on as she did.

She was also, he noticed, very soft. Soft to the touch, soft the way a woman should be.

And joining the flame of anger in his stomach was a sudden burst of arousal that took him completely off guard. He tamped it down, ignoring it, his teeth clenched tightly together as he fought the temptation to look down at her naked body.

This was not about sex. It was about reclaiming the territory that she had attempted to stake as her own.

If he was to marry this little devil, he would have to show her that he would have the upper hand. That she would not be dictating to him.

That went for his body, as well.

He had to take utter control, of her, of himself. There was no other option. He would have to be firm with her. Starting now.

"Let us get one thing straight," he said. "This is not a hotel. This is my bedroom. This," he added, tossing her down with no gentleness whatsoever onto the center of his bed, "is my bed. I do two things in this bed. I have sex and I sleep. If you intend to *stay* in my bed, you will partake in both of those things with me. Otherwise feel free to find a more suitable accommodation."

Again, he resisted the temptation to look at her body, though he imagined she was currently spread out for him like a particularly delectable buffet. But he intended to scare her off, not violate her in any way.

She wasn't still for long. She scrambled across the mattress and buried herself beneath the blankets, shielding her body from his view. "You," she said, her voice shaking, "are terrible."

"We are to be married," he said. "Nothing I've done or said should be all that shocking." He knew full well he was being shocking; he just didn't care.

"I don't know you."

"But you will know me quite well in only a couple of months' time. We could start now."

"We shall not!"

"Then you shall vacate my bedroom. I find that I am quite tired." He reached up, grabbing hold of the knot on his tie and loosening it.

Her eyes went wide, her hands curling tightly around the white comforter on his bed, digging sharply into the material like claws. "You wouldn't," she said, her shocked tone spurring him on all the more.

He kept his eyes on hers as he tugged his tie off and cast it to the floor before undoing the top button on his shirt. "As I said, I find I am quite tired. This is my bed. I have already given you the list of activities performed therein."

He undid a second button on his shirt and watched as her eyes grew even rounder. He undid another, then another, moving closer and closer to the bed. He found his own heart was starting to pound harder. He would not touch her. He knew this would end with her running away before he had to. Still, that didn't stop the blood from firing harder and faster through his veins.

His mind might be well aware that he was a modern man who would never take advantage of a woman in such a way, but his body clearly hadn't gotten the memo. All he knew was that he was a man, and she was a woman. A very beautiful woman.

And in that moment he started to forget exactly what he was doing here.

He undid yet another button on his shirt, and suddenly she rolled to the side, wrapping the blanket around her body and landing on the floor. She stood up, the blankets concealing her curves. Her dark hair was wet, stringy and partly covering her face. And with all that, she was still trying to look imperious. "All right. You may arrange separate quarters for me." She turned to the side, kicking the excess fabric from the comfort her out of her way. "I am going to dress. When I return I expect for things to be arranged."

He laughed at her retreating form, and her shoulders grew stiff, her frame all but vibrating with rage.

He took his phone out of his pocket and made a call to his brother's chief of staff, letting him know that the princess was ready to be shown to her room. Zara returned before the staff came to escort her away. She was dressed in a pair of soft pink pajamas that looked as though they belonged on a much younger, much less venomous girl.

"Am I leaving soon?" she asked.

"Listen to you. Quite impatient to go now."

"You make a very persuasive argument."

He chuckled again, amusement at her open hostility irresistible. He was not used to this reaction from women. But then, he was not used to being engaged to a woman. A woman who clearly didn't want to be engaged to him any more than he wanted to be betrothed to her. "Most women don't run away from me when I start taking my shirt off."

Her lip curled. "I am not most women, you will find."

He rubbed his chin, eyeing her figure, certainly not displayed to any advantage by the flannel she was currently wearing. "This may be a problem, as I expect you to be very like a woman when it comes to our marriage. You must be both a wife to me and a suitable public display for my country." And he had to be the prince his brother needed him to be.

"I am unsuitable," she said, far too quickly.

"And yet my brother says you *are* suitable. The only suitable choice, in fact. So there we have a problem." He regarded her even more closely. Her dark eyes were glittering, and for the first time he saw that there was quite a deep well of fear beneath her prickly exterior. For the first time he questioned the way he had handled her. He was angry at being maneuvered, and he was taking his anger out on her. But she was not a part of this, any more than he was. "You have nothing to fear from me. You have nothing to fear from Kairos, even though he can come across as quite the tyrant. Neither of us is going to hurt you."

He saw no signs of relief on her face. "But you are going to use me," she said.

"You are royalty, Zara. Had you not been thrown out of the palace as a child and spirited away to live with the Gypsies, you would certainly be facing an arranged marriage anyway. Just as I expected I would be one day, though not quite with such short notice."

"Don't you dare lecture me on the responsibility of royalty. My life as a royal was stolen from me."

"And here you have it back. The price of admission into the life is marriage."

"I did not expect it," she said, her tone stiff.

"Did you ever expect to marry?"

She blinked. "I'm only twenty-one."

"Not so young in your country. So I ask you again, did you ever expect to marry?"

She lifted her shoulder. "Were I a typical part of the clan I was raised in, I would likely be married by now. But I was not. I was under their protection. So different things were expected."

"Is that your very long, uninteresting way of saying you did not expect to marry?"

Her expression darkened. "I may have someday. But I was in hiding to spare my own life, in order to save myself from a fate such as this. I hadn't given it much thought. I knew I would have to leave if I was ever going to pursue a normal existence…"

"I suppose this isn't exactly normal."

"Indeed."

"You will need to be trained," he said.

Her frown deepened. "Oh, really?"

"Yes. I think it's entirely possible for you to be made into a suitable bride. You have the looks for it. You simply need…taming."

"Am I so wild?"

"You have no sense of decorum. Your burrowing into my room is evidence of that. Your hair, your posture… You exude."

"I exude what?"

He let out a long, slow breath. "You exude. In general that isn't something a princess should do. You need to be…placid. Serene. As I said before, tame."

She clenched her hands into fists, her expression filled with rage. Her dark hair hung lank down her back, making her look all the more wild. "I refuse to be tamed."

He wasn't entirely sure what to say to that, and he resented her for making him feel as if his back were up against a wall. Kairos had given his orders, and Andres had sins he needed to atone for.

Part of him wondered why he was making an effort. He failed, that was what he did. Their father had always been quick to remind him of that fact when they were boys, and still when they were men. Kairos was the responsible one, the heir, thankfully, as he took his role so very seriously. Andres had been the one his father could always count on to create a scandal, to make a mess, to create disaster.

There was a reason he'd been barred from official events as a child. Reasons he had spent state dinners locked in his room while the rest of the family put on a show.

Their father might be dead now, but the feel of his cold eyes on Andres remained. Of the hard disappointment that had laced every word the old man had ever spoken to him.

He had given Kairos his word, and he would not fail. Not again. In this, he would triumph.

It was only marriage. And she was only a woman. How could he lose?

He was a legendary playboy renowned for his

skills of seduction. Surely he could seduce this scraggly waif easily enough.

"You will not refuse me," he said. "What is it you want, anything besides freedom? I will see that you have it. Surely there must be something. Surely we can trade."

She looked down, hesitating for a moment. "I wish to be sure my people are cared for. Beyond that, that those who raised me are safe."

"Then those will be the conditions of us forging trade alliances with Tirimia. You will have much more power here, on this throne, than you will have hiding in the forest back in your homeland. That I can promise you. You will have the ear of the king who is both good and just. You will be a princess in her rightful place. Surely that is better than hiding in a burrow like a little mouse."

She frowned, her dark eyebrows drawn tightly together, a crease forming between them. "You are fond of comparing me to animals."

"You are closer to animal than human female at the moment, sadly for me." And he was much closer to a wolf than a man. "So you will allow me to fashion you into a suitable bride. In return, I will give you what you want." There was a knock on the door to his bedchamber. "That will be the servants, ready to take you to your room."

She nodded slowly. "All right."

Some of the fire had gone out of her in the past few minutes. He found he did not like it.

That makes no sense.

No, it didn't. But nothing about the past twelve hours made any sense at all.

"We start tomorrow. Meet me in the general study after breakfast."

"What are you going to do?"

"Tame you, of course."

CHAPTER FOUR

IT TURNED OUT that Andres's definition of taming her actually meant attempting to smother her in yards of silk and tulle.

She did not feel tame in the least. Instead, she felt slightly indignant and more than a little bit irritated. Though that had been her state of being since he threw her out of his bedchamber last night.

Just thinking about it sent a hot flush over her skin, exacerbated by the cool slide of the silk that was currently being fitted to her form. She assumed the rash of heat was brought about by anger. She was angry. The way he had plucked her out of the bath, holding her against him, as though he had every right to touch her, as though she belonged to him in some way, was nothing less than enraging.

Except it didn't feel like any rage she had ever experienced before. But then, she was in a palace unlike any she'd ever been in before, wearing clothes the likes of which she had never even dreamed up before, so she imagined that was in keeping with the theme.

"Keep your shoulders straight," the seamstress

said, her tone stiff, as stiff as Zara's shoulders were starting to feel.

"You heard her," Andres's voice came from beyond the screen she was standing behind. "Keep still, or it will take longer."

"I am not a child," she said, addressing both of them. "I don't need to be spoken to like one."

"Then do not fidget like one," the woman said.

Zara fought the urge to fidget just to cause trouble.

This was very strange, being the focus like this. The closest experience she had in her memory was when she had come to live at the encampment. She had been a curiosity then, but they had also been careful with her. She was a little girl who had lost her family, who was traumatized, steeped in grief.

Resources there were limited, and no one had ever procured her a new wardrobe. She'd had clothing crudely fitted to her before. Hand-me-downs that she'd acquired within the camp.

In her life before the revolution, she was certain she had experienced things like this, but there was a veil drawn over those years, memories she found difficult to access. Everything was reduced down to feelings. Still pictures in her mind. Smells, tastes.

She'd only been six when she was taken away.

So much more of her life spent away from the palace than in it.

She was trying to hate it, but in truth it was difficult. The dress she was wearing at the moment was irresistible. She had never imagined she would find a dress irresistible, but she definitely had strong feelings about this one.

The bodice was fitted, soft with iridescent pink vines stitched over the silk. The skirt billowed around her like a pink cloud. And in truth, she would love to hate it for its impracticality. But it was just too pretty.

Though, even if she was having a hard time resenting the dress, she could still easily resent Andres.

"Would you like to see this one, Your Highness?" The woman spoke to Andres as though Zara weren't standing right there.

"Why not?" He sounded bored, which she found insulting. Though, had he sounded eager, she probably would have been similarly offended. He could not win with her. She had decided.

She would not allow him to. She would not marry him. She would find another way.

Though it has been said you catch more flies with honey than vinegar. And you need his help.

She ignored that thought. Yes, it was true she needed him in some capacity. But she would not be pouring out the kind of honey a man like him wanted. Andres had not been ambiguous about his intent for her. He'd told her last night that if she didn't leave he was going to...

She felt her skin growing hot again, just as the seamstress moved the screen to the side, removing the buffer that stood between herself and the rather imposing prince.

She drew in a deep breath, her breasts pushing against the tight, structured bodice. She was very conscious of the fact that his eyes were very much focused on said part of her body. He was doing it to make her uncomfortable. There was no other reason. Men did not waste time staring at her chest. Men did not waste time staring at any part of her.

Yes, she had been well protected, prior to being kidnapped and returned to the palace to be used as a political pawn, but it had not seemed to be a particular challenge for the leader of their clan to keep men away from her.

Quite the opposite, Zara felt sometimes as if she repelled people when she walked through a crowd.

The heat in his eyes was certainly not real. Which made it all the more offensive, even if it should have made it less offensive. Things with Andres simply weren't going to make sense, she had accepted that already.

"Well?" she asked, the word coming out as a command.

He put his hand on his chin as though he were considering. "You certainly look more like a princess than you did yesterday."

"I suppose it depends on your cultural point of view," she said, raising an eyebrow.

"Indeed?"

"Yes. Among my people the gold makeup is considered the mark of royalty. A mark of beauty. The robe I wore yesterday, the purple with gold thread signified that, as well. This is just a pretty dress."

"This is *couture*," the seamstress said, speaking out of turn, her tone harsh.

"Will you allow her to speak to me like that?" Zara asked.

"Yes. You were offensive," Andres said.

"My apologies," she said, not feeling particularly apologetic. It was difficult when she still felt maneuvered. Forced. Imprisoned. "I am tired." She lifted up the heavy, voluminous skirts and turned, sitting on the edge of the bed, the fabric billowing around her.

"Yes. I imagine trying on gowns all day is incredibly taxing," he said, his tone dry.

"Is it perhaps as taxing as sitting there watching someone else do it?"

"Probably not as taxing as measuring a fidgeting, surly girl." He leaned against the wall, crossing his arms over his chest, his expression laconic. "Elena," he said, addressing the seamstress, "I'm sure you could use a break. The princess and I can handle things from here."

"Yes, Your Highness." The woman was clearly unhappy with being dismissed, leaving her dresses behind for someone other than her to handle. But she obeyed.

Zara didn't think she would ever get used to that. The fact that ultimately Andres would have to be deferred to, and beyond him Kairos. She fell somewhere beneath the two of them.

It isn't as though you had any power back in the encampment. People put you on a pedestal, but you had no choices.

She ignored herself again, focusing instead on the growing sense of dread she felt as Elena walked out of the room, leaving her alone with Andres.

"So?" She lifted her hands, then brought them back down, gripping the fabric of the gown. "Am I suitably altered into your preferred image?"

"You have a ways to go yet," he said, his tone dry. "You still look a bit wild."

"Perhaps because I am a bit wild. Have you ever thought that no amount of work will change that? No matter how sleek you make me look, it will not change what's inside?"

"As far as I'm concerned, outward appearance is the best place to start. Changing who you are on the inside is a much more difficult task."

"Speaking from experience?"

One side of his mouth curved upward. "Experience at not managing to change it, certainly."

"If you haven't managed to change after all your years of living in this palace, what makes you think you will manage to change me and in only a couple of months?"

"I don't have to change you, not really. I only have to make it look as though you have changed. And *that*, I have ample experience with."

"I thought the ultimate goal was taming."

The other corner of his mouth turned up, and he was smiling now. Yet she didn't get the sense that there was any humor in it. "Let me ask you this. Do you think I am tame?"

She looked him over, at the perfectly tailored lines of his suit, the aristocratic cut of his features. He could have been carved, rather than made. A Greek statue with life breathed into it, rather than a man born of a woman.

He was beautiful. She found nothing feminine about the descriptor. She would call the forest, the mountains back in Tirimia beautiful, while they were, at the same time, uncompromising and dangerous. She had a feeling Andres was both of those things in addition to being beautiful. His brother, Kairos, exuded danger, authority. With Andres it was less immediately apparent.

But she could see it. She could sense it.

Possibly that was due more to the fact that he had pulled her out of the bathtub yesterday and thrown her onto his bed, than any kind of sixth sense on her part.

Still, she was confident in her answer to his question.

"No. You aren't," she said.

"But I appear to be. Or rather, I appear to be when it suits me."

"Is that what you are suggesting I do? Behave the part of princess in public?"

"I should like for you to be a little bit more tame than you already are, as I have no interest in being bitten." Something changed in his eyes as he said the words. Anger morphing into something else entirely. To a molten heat she could swear radiated from him. Something she couldn't quite sort out. There was a lot of that between them.

"I have never bitten anyone in my life. Your concerns are unfounded."

He arched an eyebrow. "Are they?" He took a step toward her, his dark eyes boring into hers. "If I were to grab you now and throw you down on that bed, you wouldn't bite me?"

Her heart was fluttering so fast she could

scarcely catch her breath. "Why would you do that?"

"Do not tell me you are so naive that you are unaware of what a man wants from a woman," he said, something hard, dangerous in his tone.

"Of course not," she said, her throat feeling tight, her face hot.

"You know what a husband wants from his wife, then," he said.

It felt as if a fire had broken out over her body, burning her in the most intimate places. She should strangle him with his own tie for daring to speak to her in such a manner. She should certainly not be overheating. "But I am not your wife."

He reached out, taking her chin between his thumb and forefinger, his hold firm, his eyes locked with hers. She should move away from him. She should kick him. She did neither.

"You will be my wife. In every sense of the word. I do like that dress," he said, his gaze roaming over her body. "I do wonder, though, if I would like it better on the floor." He leaned in closer, and her breath caught. "I wonder, if I stripped it from your body, if I were to try and claim you, would you try to bite me then?"

"Try it," she said, her voice trembling, "try it and see, you bastard."

"Dirty talk. I like it. If you think that's going

to push me away, I hate to disappoint you." He moved closer then, his lips a whisper away from hers. And she found that rather than wanting to draw away, perversely she wanted to lean in closer to him. She could feel a connection forming between them, physical, real, tangible. She wanted to solidify it. She didn't want to break it. How long had it been since she felt connected to anyone? How long had it been since anyone touched her? "Sadly, for you, disappointing people is what I do best."

Then he moved away. She felt his withdrawal like a gale-force wind. Making her feel disheveled, cold.

"I resisted the urge to eviscerate you with my teeth," she said, trying to keep her tone stiff. "Perhaps I am not as uncivilized as you seem to think I am."

"Perhaps I'm not as *civilized* as you think I am."

"If you're trying to frighten me into submitting to your marriage plan, I'm afraid I must deliver the disappointing news that it will not work." She swallowed hard, calling on all her strength to form the next sentence, to meet his gaze while she spoke the words.

He laughed, a dark, humorless sound. "Silly woman. I don't need your submission. I need your cooperation."

"Is there any way I can help you without marrying you?"

"No. There isn't."

She gritted her teeth. "That's very inflexible of you."

"I am inflexible. In this instance largely because my brother is. I owe him. I disappointed him once, and I cannot do it again. This is my atonement. You are my penance."

"I suppose in that case lowering yourself onto my body will be much like crawling over broken glass."

He chuckled, which angered her because those words had cost her. Because she was dealing in subject matter she was not well versed in, trying to play that she was sophisticated. As if the things he said were unremarkable. And when she reached for a comment she thought might shock him, he didn't even have the decency to look fazed. "To the contrary, I imagine lowering myself onto your body—as you so eloquently put it—will be the most enjoyable portion of our enforced union."

"Why marriage?" she asked, feeling desperate. "Why not… I suppose I don't understand what else I could do, because I'm not entirely certain why it is you need me."

"I must marry you because Kairos gave the order for me to do so. Kairos asked me to do so to improve relations between Petras and Tirimia. Presumably there are more detailed explanations available, but he didn't give them, and I didn't ask. The reasoning was irrelevant."

"And yet you do not seem like a man who would normally feel that way. I can't imagine that you're docilely lying down and engaging in something against your will, simply because it's the right thing to do. There is something else to this. There has to be."

She had no idea how she was so certain of this, only that she was. Nothing about Andres was docile. She was right, he wasn't tame. Not in the least. And yet he was allowing himself to be collared and muzzled by his older brother. It made no sense.

"I told you already I spent a great many years doing nothing less than exactly what I wanted. In fact, I was doing that only last week. I have made mistakes," he said, his tone uncompromising. "Mistakes I had hoped were healed by time, and circumstance that had nothing to do with conciliatory actions on my part. It turns out I was wrong."

"Be specific," she said. "Where I come from we don't deal in this kind of circular conversation. Either we tell someone what we are thinking, or we don't. There is no alluding to events and talking around the most important element of the truth."

It was true, though she was rarely included in important conversations back in her homeland. Still, the exclusion was not ambiguous.

"You want to know what I did? Is that it?"

"If it answers the question of why you're doing this, then yes. I feel like I have a right to know."

"So be it, then."

Andres felt strangely reluctant to tell Zara the truth. It was an oddity that she didn't know already. Everyone in his country did. Anyone abroad who read tabloids while standing in line at the grocery store knew the sordid details of his past, and what had become of Kairos's first engagement.

And it was that fact that made him so reluctant to speak of it.

She didn't look at him and see the playboy prince. Didn't look at him and see the black sheep. She didn't like him, but that was based entirely on the interactions they'd had, not on any rumor or headline.

Strange that he found that refreshing, but he did.

Strange that he should care at all what she thought. But he did. He had made a practice of shedding outside opinion from an early age. When he'd first come back from the shadows and into the public eye as a teenager.

"I get the feeling you don't read a lot of gossip news."

"No," she said.

He sat down in the chair opposite her, affecting a casual posture. He was a professional at pretending not to care, particularly at moments when he cared quite a bit. "Then you won't have read about my escapades. They're legendary. There isn't a woman I can't seduce. No supermodel with sex on her mind I've ever refused. I always leave them wanting more, as I rarely stay with a woman for more than one night. I have no shame. No morals to speak of whatsoever."

He watched as the color in her cheeks rose, turning a dark pink that matched the embroidery on her dress. "Is that so?" Her voice was husky, her eyes focused somewhere on the wall behind him. He couldn't work her out. Was she simply uncomfortable in his presence, angry and biding her time, or did she feel the insistent tug of attraction just as he did?

He had been with a great many women. And while he wasn't particularly proud of that behavior when he stood back and took stock of it, it could not be denied. With his vast experience it made no sense that he would be tempted by this woman. She was not sophisticated. She was beautiful, but a great many women were beautiful. Beautiful without being too sharp, too fearsome and too wild.

She was like the wind, bottled up and stitched into a gown. He had to wonder if she had allowed for herself to be harnessed and was simply waiting for the right moment to free herself again.

"Yes. The media always said I had no shame. I imagine that I must have some, though I have not felt any in quite some time. It's very liberating," he said, not sure why he was adding this to the conversation, "to feel no embarrassment. To feel no compunction about simply acting on your impulses because you have accepted that you are capable of nothing else. Still, I didn't imagine that I was absent of shame entirely. That isn't true of anyone except for sociopaths. And I never *thought* that I was a sociopath. Then my brother and I, and his fiancée, Francesca, flew to Monte Carlo for a bit of fun and games. Kairos, being Kairos, was having fun in a very dignified manner. Largely he was meeting with world leaders in a more casual environment. I was there to have real fun. And so, it turned out, was Francesca. While Kairos was out I threw a party in my suite. I invited every beautiful woman I could find, every man interested in engaging in a bit of gambling and debauchery. There was a lot of alcohol, as there invariably is at these things. It turns out, the right amount of alcohol is all it takes for me to lose my last vestiges of shame. It was at this party that I proved the media right."

"What did you do?" Her question, confused, mystified, enhanced by those wide dark eyes, shamed him in a way nothing else ever had. She truly couldn't guess. Couldn't even fathom the betrayal he was about to uncover for her.

Yes, if she was going to be his wife, it was best she understood now. Just who he was. Just what he was.

What your parents always knew you were.

"I screwed my brother's fiancée. I wouldn't even have remembered if it had not been for videos of the event. Not only did I humiliate my brother, but I made both Francesca and myself porn stars. That did not go over well with her family, if you were wondering. Nor did it go over well with mine."

Those wide eyes now registered shock, horror. He was torn between the disappointment of watching her understand, of seeing her accept the reality of what he was, and a strange fascination that he could still shock someone. That she hadn't somehow sensed upon their first meeting that he was flawed in a very real and insurmountable way. In a way he had fully embraced. He was not a man capable of doing things by halves. And since he could not be good, then he had purposed to be debauched to his very core.

He had a feeling that if he tried to explain that to Zara she would look at him as though he had grown another head. He was struck just then at how different their lives had been. He lived in a different world. The moment he'd gained control of his life, he'd made it exactly what he'd wanted. One filled with parties, as much human contact as he wanted. A different woman every night, helping to fill the void that might have been tempted to widen inside him if he allowed it.

She had lived a much more solitary existence. While his had been cluttered with noise. As much as he could possibly surround himself with.

They might as well have been from other planets entirely.

"Now," he said, not seeing the point in continuing the discussion. "You will tell me something about yourself."

She tilted her chin up, her expression proud. "The fact that I witnessed my family's death isn't enough information for you?"

Something uncomfortable, heavy, shifted in his chest. "You don't want to marry me," he said.

"Of course not."

"Why not?"

"Aside from the fact that you're a stranger, you just confessed to me that you betrayed your brother. You... You just told me you were the most faithless man on the planet, and now you're seriously asking me why I don't want to marry you?"

"You said yourself you had no plans to marry. Don't tell me now that you had fantasies of a white picket fence and a husband who only had eyes for you. Our marriage could be whatever you want it to be, but you haven't even asked me what my designs on you are. You haven't asked me what my goal is for our union, haven't given any input on how you would like things to be conducted. You simply don't want to marry me. Which makes me think you must have a goal apart from me."

She looked away, her jaw set, stubborn.

"Answer me, feral creature, or I will make good on my earlier threat."

"Listen to you," she said, her head whipping around, her lip contorted into a sneer, "the man who just professed to being able to seduce any woman is threatening me with his body."

"You would be seduced soon enough." He ground his teeth together. "And I might even find I don't mind being bitten."

"I don't wish to get my mouth dirty."

He laughed, though he felt no amusement. "I will remember that. Now, tell me. I grow impatient."

"I too am impatient, and yet no one seems concerned about that. I have been held captive for the past two months, before my ownership was transferred to you. Yes, I find I am quite impatient. I've never had any say in my life. I was born into royalty, in a position more vulnerable than I could ever have imagined when surrounded by the stone walls of the palace. Then I lost everyone and was taken away to the middle of the forest. Then I was taken captive. And now I have been delivered to you, to be your wife, and I have no choice, yet again. Who am I? What am I to be? The pawn of whoever holds me in their hand at any given time? I must be more than that, Andres. I should like a chance to find out."

Her words touched something in him. Strange, because nothing about her should resonate. They were different. From different worlds, as he had only just been thinking. Somehow he recognized these words as though they had originated in his own head.

"You will," he said. "That is another promise I make to you. Our marriage does not have to be traditional in any sense. Not if you don't wish it. In truth, I am not suited to forsaking all others. It is simply not in me. If I have a certain measure of freedom, then you will too."

"What are you suggesting?"

"After you have our children you will be free to pursue lovers as you see fit. Or to pursue different hobbies and interests. Education if you wish."

"Interesting that you prioritize lovers over education."

"*I* would certainly choose lovers over education. But it is your choice."

She frowned. "Why?"

"Why what? Why am I offering you a choice? It does not benefit me to act as your prison guard. Neither do I have any desire to. I told you already, I don't particularly want a wife. But I owe Kairos. You understand now, clearly, I should think. All he requires is that we produce a child who can take the throne should he and his wife be unable to fulfill the task."

"I see. You only need my womb. As if that isn't an extremely large thing to ask."

"It would be a family. Blood. How long has it been since you've been a part of that?" He hated himself for using this against her. Still, he was a man with no shame, and he was hardly going to grow any on the spot.

She looked away.

"A long time," he answered for her. "Do not fight against me. Neither of us has a choice. We do not need it to be any more difficult than it already is."

He stood, getting ready to go.

"Can you call the seamstress back?"

It was not what he expected her to say. But then, he found he could not predict Zara. She didn't fall neatly into a category the way the women he often associated with did. "What do you need?"

"I'm not going to be able to get myself out of this," she said, indicating her gown.

"I am more than willing to help you with that, Princess," he said.

Heat formed a ball in his gut, a knot he could barely breathe past. Here he was, talking to her about taking other lovers once they took their vows, and yet he was getting aroused by the thought of unzipping her dress. He'd helped countless women out of couture gowns; there should be nothing exceptional about this moment. Nothing particularly interesting about this desire. And yet there was.

"No, you cannot." Her voice was stiff, her obvious distress indicating that she was not immune to him either.

"You would rather call Elena back in here just to unzip you? Seems a bit much. Do I frighten you so intensely?"

Something flared in her dark eyes. "Nothing frightens me. I already told you once. How quickly you forget."

"Then turn around."

She obeyed, and he knew it was out of sheer stubbornness more than anything else. He reached out, gripping the tab on the dress, drawing it down slowly, ignoring the slight tremble in his fingers. There was no reason for him to tremble. He was unveiling nothing more than the elegant length of her spine. Beautiful, certainly, as everything about her was, but unremarkable.

One of many naked female backs he had seen.

She looked over her shoulder, and lust hit him square and hard in the stomach. Her eyes were like no one else's.

And it didn't matter how many women he had undressed in the past, because they hadn't been her. Because it wasn't now.

Dammit, he had to get a grip.

When he had the zipper lowered all the way he took a step back, forcing his hands down at his side so he wouldn't grip the sides of the bodice and pull it down, past her hips, to pool on the floor. So that he didn't lose hold of his very tenuous control and do exactly what he had threatened to do earlier.

"Go now," she said, the words quivering.

"As you wish, Princess. But there will come a time when I don't leave once your clothes come off." He didn't know why he felt the need to add that. Didn't know why he always felt the need to get in one more hit. Perhaps because he was powerless, as was the situation in many ways. She was too. Which is perhaps why she felt the need to lash out at him.

It was why he kept striking out at her.

"Not a day sooner than necessary," she said.

"Get your sleep. Tomorrow you have yet more manners to learn."

"Will you make your best effort at getting me to bite you again?"

"No. Tomorrow I'm going to teach you to dance."

CHAPTER FIVE

FIRST, THEY HAD cut her hair. She couldn't recall the last time she'd had a haircut. For years she had allowed it to grow, hanging thick and curling past her waist, restrained most commonly by a braid. The palace stylist had taken it up to the middle of her back. It felt strange. A weight removed she hadn't been aware she'd been carrying.

After that, they had done her makeup. Entirely different from the way she had been taught to apply her own. But the woman had dusted the corners of Zara's eyes with gold powder, after rimming them in black, giving a different twist to the look Zara was accustomed to. A sort of marriage between Tirimian standards of beauty and those here in Petras.

Her gown, the third piece of her early-morning makeover, was another example of that.

Unlike the frothy confection she had worn yesterday, this gown was sleek, hugging her curves. Gold beadwork stitched onto filmy fabric that ended at her knees, turning to sheer netting past that point that was also made to glitter with the same golden details.

Her newly cut hair had been styled into glossy waves. She had never imagined her hair could look quite like this. Usually it looked much more...natural. Rough-hewn. Usually *she* looked much more rough-hewn.

She had the distinct feeling Andres would see it as a victory.

The thought would have irritated her more if she weren't so fascinated by her own reflection. Sadly she didn't have very long to linger over the stranger in the mirror. She had to go down to the ballroom because Andres was intent on teaching her to dance.

Just thinking of him made her stomach tighten, and the feeling only increased as she made her way down the stairs, down the corridor that would lead her to the ballroom. In theory. She had never been in the palace's ballroom before. She had been given rather simple directions, and since she could easily find her way through a forest, she imagined she could navigate her way through a castle.

She paused at the ornate double doors that separated the corridor from the room, and her, presumably, from Andres. This was her last moment to take a breath of air before he was standing in front of her, tightening her lungs.

She breathed in deeply, then took a step forward, grabbing hold of the handle and pulling, the heavy door giving slowly. She slipped through the open space and stopped, taking in the grand sight before her. The ceiling was high, domed, with beautiful, detailed paintings stretching over the width of the room. The walls were papered a pale blue with crushed velvet flowers, each segment of wall divided by golden molding.

She would blend in with these surroundings. A strange thought. But it was true. Now she looked as though she belonged here. Felt as though she might. She was born to this. Would have lived in it if not for the men who'd overthrown her father.

This would have been her birthright. And in reality, she would very likely have been sent to marry a prince. A prince like Andres.

This could have been her fate no matter what. To be here. To be with him. Set to be his wife. Such a strange thought. But comforting in some ways. Was this what her parents would have planned for her? They certainly wouldn't have wanted her to stay in the woods for the rest of her life.

She had been… She closed her eyes for a moment, taking a deep breath. It smelled familiar here. Of ancient stone and wood. A palace. It reminded her of her home. Her first home. Of her parents and how they had cared for her.

They had loved her. So very much. This was the sort of life they had wanted for her. The woman she was now, in the dress she currently wore, was what they would have wanted her to be.

Had she been brought up in the palace, she would be tamed already rather than being something he saw as a feral animal.

Zara swallowed. She should not care about that. What he thought of her. She wasn't actually going to marry him. She would find a way out of this. Find a way to make it work for everyone.

She was not ready to be married. Least of all to a man who had as little choice in the matter as she did.

She had been forced into too many things. Had been forced on too many people. Was it such a bad thing to wish she could be chosen?

She shook off the thought, walking deeper into the room. It was silly to worry about things like that. Being chosen, and wanted. Those were luxuries for people who didn't have to worry about survival, or about duty.

It would not have fit into either versions of her life.

Andres chose that moment to walk in the doors opposite her. She would have expected to be used to him by now. Would have thought that every time she saw him the impact of his appearance would lessen. If anything, she felt it harder, deeper, every time she saw him. He was dressed in a tuxedo, and she could have almost laughed at the absurdity of it. Her in a ball gown, him in a suit, so early in the day, in an empty ballroom.

Two strangers who were being ordered to marry each other, neither of whom wanted to.

She would have laughed, but she couldn't possibly. Not when she could scarcely even take a breath. If she had felt tense at the mere thought of seeing Andres, then actually seeing him ratcheted her tension up to impossible degrees. She couldn't figure out why. Yes, he was handsome, but she had no interest in being touched by him. Being kissed by him. Or any of those other things.

She had never much minded being innocent for her age. A side effect of being kept separate from everyone else was most certainly innocence. There had been no boys to hold her hand, kiss her, during her teenage years. There had been no one to talk to her about relationships. Everything she knew she had gathered by listening and observing. And that—up until now—had been enough. Now she felt out of her depth. Confused and, worst of all, curious. Curious about what it would be like if he made good on any of his threats. Curious about what he looked like beneath those suits. Beneath that facade he wore so casually and easily she doubted most people recognized it as such. But she did. She knew what it was like to put a veneer over everything you were. To keep your manner calm, unshakable, while underneath a storm raged.

They were so very different, and yet she could

see reflections of herself in his dark eyes. It made no sense. It made even less sense than her fascination with him. It should be fear. She could not deny that her feelings were certainly tinged with it, but that wasn't all of it.

Yes, it was the curiosity that disturbed her the most. If she had even a few more answers to her questions, perhaps it would not be. If she had been with a man before, or at least been kissed by one, then perhaps she wouldn't be so fascinated by the shape of his mouth. Perhaps she wouldn't have so many questions about whether or not it would be as hot, firm, certain, as it looked.

He looked up, his eyes meeting hers. And he stopped. Froze, right there in the middle of the room, staring at her as though she were a foreign entity.

"You've cut your hair," he said.

She reached up, touching the silken length. "Well, *I* didn't."

"The stylist did."

"Yes." She flicked the dark curl over her shoulder. "Am I not tame?"

He tilted his head to the side. "I'm not sure. Why don't you come closer and I'll try to assess for myself?"

She found herself obeying, moving toward him warily, not quite sure why.

Perhaps it was all to do with lulling him into a

false sense of security. Getting him to trust her. Yes, that was likely the reason. It had nothing to do with the tightness in her stomach, the pressure on her lungs, the dry feeling in her throat. Had nothing to do with the deadly beauty he possessed. Like a rugged landscape that beckoned you to explore, while waiting to swallow you whole.

None of that mattered. It meant nothing. It was only that fighting the entire way wouldn't help her cause, so there was no purpose in it. She had to wait and strike when it counted. So she would obey. But only for now.

It was his turn to touch her hair. He reached out slowly, and she could do nothing more than watch as he reached for her as he rubbed his thumb over the dark, silken locks. He said nothing; he only stared.

She wanted to ask if he liked it, but she realized that she shouldn't care whether he liked it or not. She didn't need him to find her beautiful; she needed him to find her sympathetic. It would probably work to her advantage if he didn't find her beautiful.

No matter how compelling he was, no matter how handsome, it didn't change what he was. He had told her in no uncertain terms. He had betrayed his brother. Not out of any real need, or great affection and love for the woman in question. Just because he could. Just because he lived to please himself. That, more than anything, should repel her. Should make his opinion on her appearance moot.

When she thought of her mother and father, of what they'd done with their positions, the changes they had died for…it should make him repellent. That he had such power and did nothing with it.

It didn't.

How disappointing to discover that she was as vulnerable to this kind of thing as any other woman.

Suddenly, he changed their positions, wrapping his arm around her waist and taking hold of her hand with his. "We're here to dance," he said. "Do you know how?"

She knew that he had asked a question, and that the question required a response, but she couldn't seem to cobble one together. He was strong. She had known that. He had plucked her out of the bathtub and carried her across the room as though she weighed nothing. Still, she had forgotten somehow. Or she hadn't fully realized. Or perhaps the memory simply couldn't do it justice.

He was strong, yes, but the true test of that was the way he held her without crushing her. Firm, but gentle. She could feel the heat of his skin radiating through the fabric of his suit, had a sense for the hard muscle beneath. So much only hinted at. Another piece of evidence to support her theory that he was hiding his real self beneath a mask.

"Put your hand on my shoulder," he said.

She obeyed again, because that was easier than trying to form words and actually figure out how to speak them. She felt every inch the creature he had accused her of being on multiple occasions. Completely ill-equipped to handle interaction with a man. As though she really had been raised by wolves and not just by a family who had a simpler lifestyle.

"You don't know how to dance," he said, answering his earlier question for her.

She shook her head, trying not to focus on the places where his hands were making contact. The way his fingers were laced through hers, the way his palm rested on her lower back. This didn't feel as if she was going along with it simply to keep him sweet. This felt like something else. It was confusing. Terrifying.

It couldn't happen.

Attraction had no place in any of this. It had no place in her life, not until she figured out what she wanted her life to look like. How could she even begin to answer that question until she got to know herself better? For some reason, standing in the center of this ballroom, held tightly in his arms, she was so acutely aware of how thin her life experiences had been until now. Every single thing was tied to her title. A title she had never been able to claim or use.

But oh, how she had suffered for it. The realization should feel...desolate. But for some reason, standing there in his arms, it was cushioned. Perhaps because someone was finally touching her. She finally felt connected. And so she asked him.

"Do you like my hair?" She couldn't bring herself to look at his face in case she caught him in a lie.

"Yes," he said, the answer slow, cautious. "Though I quite liked it before. There is something captivating about the wilder aspects you carry, I must confess."

She couldn't stop herself from looking up at him now. He was still holding her, neither of them moving. This was no way to conduct a dance lesson, and yet she found she wasn't interested in discontinuing the conversation. "What do you like about my wildness?"

"You are fierce. You fight. I can't help being compelled by that. You are everything you feel, rather than being what others should see. How can I not be intrigued by that?"

"Because you can only be what is acceptable?"

"Because I'm surrounded by people who behave themselves." It was a deflection, she was aware. He didn't deny her accusation, but he didn't admit to it either. "It is refreshing to see someone who doesn't."

"You've only seen me here. I spent a great many years behaving myself by the standards of my surroundings."

"Tell me," he said, and then he started to move. Leading her in a dance that had no music.

She held tightly to him, trying to keep from stumbling. "Tell you about my life with the clan?"

"Yes. Tell me what it meant to behave there."

"It's hard to explain. They cared for me. But I wasn't one of them." Standing in the palace, in this dress, she suddenly realized it was true. "I lived among them, but I could never say that I was accepted. Sometimes I felt as though the leader and his wife might actually... Sometimes I thought they might see me as another child... but once they had children of their own, it became very clear that wasn't the case." She'd never spoken these words out loud before. Had hardly formed them in her mind. "They were surrogate caregivers. Not a family. They observed a kind of careful distance with me, and I was expected to do the same."

"Then you didn't spend your childhood running wild?"

A smile tugged to the corner of her lips. "I did. I had all the freedom a child could wish for.

I spent a lot of time wandering through the forest on my own. Talking to myself. Talking to the trees."

"Were you lonely?" he asked, and there was a strange edge to the question, a roughness that scraped against raw places inside her.

She swallowed, ignoring the discomfort inside her. "I don't know how to answer that. It was my daily life. It was normal for me. I wasn't aware of anything missing."

It was this place, this man, that made her so aware of all she hadn't had. Of the life she *should* have lived. Of the years she'd gone without being touched.

She and Andres weren't even lovers and he touched her frequently. As though it were the most casual and easy thing.

He was touching her now. Holding her close. And she was forgetting what she was here to do. Forgetting her ultimate goal. That she was only playing along now so she could use his trust later.

Right now all she could focus on was this. The way his hands felt over the flimsy fabric of the dress. The way it felt when he said she was beautiful.

The way it felt to have a man look *at* her, not through her.

What did those things matter? What did beauty matter? It had never mattered before.

She looked away from him, trying to regain control of her thoughts. "What about you?"

"I did not wander through the woods," he said.

There was something strange in his voice. She couldn't quite place what it was. More of him not saying what he was thinking. "You weren't lonely?"

"The palace is always full of people. And these days I do love a party."

Just then, looking at him, at the stark, raw emotion that flickered in his eyes for just a moment, she was struck again by that thought she'd had about being defined by her station. Except she wondered if it had been the same for him. If he was more what his title was than who he was inside. If anyone valued him at all as a man, and not as a prince.

"That doesn't matter. The camp was always crowded. There were always people. But I was never a part of them in the same way. Families, blood family, shared space. Caravans. Sometimes they would sleep altogether around the campfire. Family is the cornerstone of the clan. And I didn't have one."

"I had a family," he said, his voice rough.

"Are your parents dead too?" It was a terribly inappropriate question, one she knew she shouldn't have asked. Andres was very careful with his words. Sometimes he was direct, tactless, but that was by choice, never on accident. Other times he was careful to make a wide circle around the point, disguising it, wrapping it in something more palatable.

But she had been raised in an environment where words weren't wasted. Where honesty, honor mattered.

Still, she regretted these words.

"My father is," he said, his tone hard. "Not my mother. At least, not as far as I know."

"She isn't here." It wasn't a question.

"She hasn't been. Not for years."

"Where did she go?"

"I, my brother, my father, and all of our Secret Service don't know the answer to that. When she disappeared, she disappeared. Not, I suspect, because she was so accomplished at subterfuge, but because she did what no one expected her to do."

"What's that?"

She expected him to stop their conversation, expected him to scold her for being too bold. Instead, a faint smile tipped the corners of his mouth upward. "I think she just walked away. With nothing but the clothes she was wearing."

"Why?" Zara had imagined doing just that. But she hadn't. Because she had no money, no identification, no skills, nothing. And yet, to hear Andres say it, it was what his mother had done.

"I suspect because it was all a bit too much for her."

"Being royal?"

He stopped moving then, but he didn't release his hold on her. "Perhaps."

There was something beneath that answer, words that weren't being spoken. He frustrated her. Made her want to pound on his chest until the truth came out. But she shouldn't care. So she didn't.

"Perhaps *I* will find it all too much," she said.

He moved without warning, releasing his hold on her hand, taking hold of her chin. "You will not leave me."

She was taken aback by the sudden intensity, by the growl in his voice. "No," she said, not entirely certain she was telling the truth.

"You dance fine," he said, releasing his hold on her and stepping away from her. The chill between them was palpable, blown in on the words she had spoken, words that had carried a power she hadn't been able to guess at.

"Thank you," she said, not really meaning it. Then she doubted he had meant what he said about her dancing.

Already, she had learned something from him. Already, she was learning to hide.

"I suggest you spend the next couple of days reflecting on the best way to present yourself to the public here in Petras. There is a traditional holiday feast at the end of the week, and we will be making our debut. It will be held here at the palace, and many of the prominent citizens here in Petras will be invited, while many more will be watching on television. My brother is going to make a speech. For some reason, the populace is very interested in what he has to say."

His mask was firmly back in place. It had slipped, only for a moment, but it had.

"I don't have to say anything, do I?" The thought had occurred to her suddenly, and had horrified her. She had never had to speak in front of people in her life.

"No. In fact, it would be best if you didn't. If you can manage to stand there, look lovely and not chew on any of the chicken bones, we should be fine."

She frowned. "I'm not going to chew on chicken bones."

"I can't be sure with you."

"What sort of debut is this, exactly?"

"You will be making your first public appearance with me. As I never bring women to such things, it will be seen as significant," he said.

She opened her mouth to protest, but before she could, he turned away from her and walked out of the room, leaving her standing there in a formal ball gown, with a sinking feeling in her stomach.

CHAPTER SIX

ZARA HAD A suspicion that her gown had been selected in an attempt to soften her appearance. Pale blue raw silk with a high neckline and a form-fitting shape that ended just below her knee. Her hair was pulled up into a bun, her makeup much more restrained than usual. Perhaps they thought that if she looked sedate she would be less likely to eat her lunch with her fingers.

Though in this case, appearances were certainly deceiving. She had reached the point of feeling quite desperate to escape this whole marriage bargain, stricken very much without her permission.

She was beginning to think that playing nice would get her nowhere. If Andres wouldn't take up her cause, she would carry it all on her own.

With flourish.

Her fingers were freezing. She was shaking a little bit, probably because she was cold. Snow had begun falling outside late last night, the temperatures plummeting. Petras bordered Greece, but was set deeper back into the mountains and had a climate that matched what she was accustomed to in Tirimia, more than their Mediterranean neighbor. Still, though she was used to the cold, for some reason it was getting to her at the moment.

It certainly wasn't nerves. It wasn't going to be difficult to sit at a table and eat food. She could manage that without humiliating anybody.

Whatever Andres thought, she wasn't an animal.

More people began to flood into the main doors of the palace, and Zara sank back into an alcove, her heart pounding heavily. She lifted her hands, clasping them together, holding her fingers tight in an attempt to warm them.

Okay, maybe she was nervous. She didn't know why. She had no stake in any of this. It had nothing to do with her.

She looked across the growing crowd and saw Andres's dark head, higher than the rest. Seeing him felt like grabbing a lifeline in the midst of the storm. She kept her eyes on him. He was familiar. A horizon line on a pitching sea.

He looked up, and their eyes locked. He changed course, parting the mass of people with his mere presence. She lowered her hands, still holding them together, trying to get a handle on her nerves.

"Where have you been?" he asked.

"Here. You didn't specify a meeting place."

"I didn't expect to find you hiding in a corner."

"I'm not hiding," she said, even though she had been doing just that.

"Kairos and Tabitha are on their way. We will walk in just after them. But before we go in, I have something for you."

She blinked, freezing, well aware that she looked a little bit as if she had been slapped upside the head. "For me?" Stupid, she was basically repeating his words back to him. But she had never been given a gift before, and she didn't quite know how to brace herself for it.

Her chest hurt. She didn't know why. She didn't know what to do about it.

It was a similar feeling to being alone in a caravan while everyone else sat outside around the fire. That, combined with the beautiful ache she felt when she was alone in the woods.

"Come here," he said.

He didn't wait for her to obey. Rather he wrapped his fingers around her arm and pulled her deeper into the corridor, around the staircase. Her breath caught as he reached into his jacket and brought out a small velvet box.

The ache in her chest split open, harsh, tearing pain now. And along with it, fear.

"No," she said.

"I never pretended this was anything but inevitable." He opened the box, and revealed exactly what she had feared. "You're acting like I'm presenting you with a tarantula, rather than a diamond ring."

She looked down at the beautiful, ornate ring. A platinum band with a large, square-cut gem at the center. She would have preferred a tarantula, frankly.

"You know how I feel about all of this. I don't… You didn't say that you were going to be making any official announcements today."

"I am bringing you to one of the most important events we have here at the palace. It is not an ambiguous statement on its own. The ring is implied."

"Then perhaps we should keep it implied," she said.

"No. That isn't how this works. I have made promises to you, promises that I intend to keep. Concessions have been made in order for you to feel as comfortable with this as possible. But you are not in charge. You are not conducting this show."

She found herself extending her hand, and she wasn't quite sure why. He had issued no threat, and truly, what would he do if she said no? Still, she held her hand there, steady for him, as he took the piece of jewelry from the box, and slipped it onto the fourth finger of her left hand. It felt heavy. And that heaviness carried over to her chest.

"Now it's time for us to go in."

He took the hand he had just put the ring on, curling his fingers around hers, leading her back toward the entrance to the ballroom. And she went. Because she was numb, and putting up a fight when you weren't entirely sure if your feet were still on the ground was difficult.

No. This wasn't what she wanted. She needed more time. She wasn't ready.

He said he would marry you by Christmas. By the end of the month. You only have a few weeks. What did you think?

She hadn't been thinking. She had been in denial of the fact that she had been brought here, given to Andres as though she were an object. A Christmas present for the man who had everything.

He had certainly taken possession of her as though he had every right. And he had made her feel as though perhaps they had a connection, but clearly they didn't. Or he could never force her into this. And he was forcing her. He *was*.

She was amazed at the way the crowd parted for him. No one touched either of them as they wove their way through the knot of people. They walked into the ballroom, toward the most opulent and beautifully appointed table. She recognized King Kairos immediately. You could hardly forget the man you'd been trotted out in front of as one of your country's desirable exports. Sitting next to him was a woman she hadn't seen yet. Blonde, poised, beautiful beyond measure. She was polished until she nearly glowed.

Suddenly, Zara could see why Andres thought she was feral.

In comparison to this woman, who had to be Queen Tabitha, almost anyone would appear feral. Her movements were fluid, her posture impeccable. Even her facial expressions seemed easy, smooth. She smiled at everyone with ease, looking perfectly genuine at every moment. Even when she rested, she simply looked serene. Never bored. Not tired, or upset.

Andres pulled her chair out for her, and she sat.

Tabitha turned her focus to Zara, and Zara saw for the first time the ice beneath the crystal-blue gaze. Tabitha was made of stronger stuff than she first appeared to be.

"Tabitha," Andres said, "this is my fiancée, Princess Zara. I'm not sure if Kairos filled you in. He played matchmaker."

Zara nearly choked.

Tabitha turned to look at her husband, her expression bland. "No. Kairos didn't tell me. I'm a bit surprised that he's responsible. He's not usually one for romance."

"Who said anything about romance?" Kairos asked.

Zara had no experience with these kinds of relationships. But she could recognize when people were circling each other. When they were holding back anger, spoiling for a fight. It was happening here.

Tabitha smiled, and this was the first time Zara could see how forced it was. The facade didn't hold up as well under close scrutiny.

She felt as though she was looking into her future. Shackled to a man who couldn't possibly be more bored with her existence. Pretending to be happy and serene when inside she wanted nothing more than to stand up and scream.

Manipulated by fate. Living a life beside someone who was entirely set apart from her.

The more she faced the possibility of a life without choice, the more she saw just how unhappy she'd been for a long time.

She'd been able to ignore it because there had always been a glimmer of hope for the future. A different future. One that was what she made it, rather than one she was forced into. And so she'd endured the silence. The distance. Because she'd imagined there would be something more later.

She looked again at Kairos and Tabitha, at the yawning gulf that was so clearly between these two people who sat right next to each other.

And then she picked up her fork. And dropped it back onto the plate. The clatter, loud and satisfying, startled everyone seated at the table. Zara smiled. "Sorry."

She wasn't sorry. Not in the least.

She wasn't going to go quietly. She wasn't going to accept this blandly. She had choices. And this was clearly a moment she had to seize. If Andres wouldn't listen to her, then she would use Kairos and Tabitha and their clear need for decorum above all else.

If he was only marrying for Kairos's sake, then she would make Kairos want her gone.

As long as they didn't return her to her captors, she would find her way.

She felt the hard, warm pressure of Andres's hand on her thigh and she turned to look at him. His eyes were hard. Warning.

But she wasn't so easily intimidated.

She returned his glare with one of her own, and a slow smile she knew he wouldn't believe sincere. "Is there a problem, Andres?"

"Not in the least," he said, his tone soft. Deceptively so.

Just as he didn't believe her smile, she did not believe his calm. "I'm pleased to hear that."

He squeezed her thigh. "You're quite docile."

She looked up at him again, fluttering her lashes. "I am. Quite."

"You had best remain so," he said, lowering his voice.

"Of course, my dear."

Moments later the waitstaff swept into the room, carrying trays laden with food. They set the small salad plates down on the larger plates. But they had to pause over hers as the fork was still sitting in the center of it. She moved it, smiling sweetly at Andres, who was eyeing her with suspicion.

He had every right to be suspicious. She was going to misbehave.

She ate the salad with very little ceremony. Not pausing in her attack of the lettuce to make polite conversation as everyone else at the table did.

She noticed Andres watching her out of the corner of his eye and lifted her thumb to her mouth to lick up a drop of dressing that wasn't really there.

Rage flared in his dark gaze, but he could do nothing. Not here. The realization sent a surge of power through her. She was unpredictable, and in this setting, that was probably quite unsettling.

"Oh," she said, watching the next trays approach. Her voice was low, and only Andres could hear her, as Tabitha and Kairos were talking to other people. "Chicken. That's delightful. I really could gnaw on the bones if I chose…"

"Do not test me, Zara," he said, his tone matching hers. "You will not like the result."

"Is that so?"

"Very."

"It seems to me," she said, eyeing her food as it was placed in front of her, "that you did not think before testing *me*. Putting a ring on my finger right before we entered the room, when I told you I wasn't ready to commit to marriage."

She reached down and picked at the piece of chicken with her fingers, keeping her eyes locked with his as she did.

He picked up her plate and in one swift movement, lowered it from the table and dumped the contents into a potted plant by the table.

"Bastard!" She whispered the invective.

"Terror," he shot back.

"I'm hungry."

No one seemed to notice what was happening, which was very annoying, since she'd intended to make a small scene. But one that looked...accidental. Not standing on chairs and causing a ruckus. She wanted to look as though she was trying to be suitable but couldn't manage it because she imagined if she made it clear she was being contrary on purpose Kairos—were he anything like his brother—would only dig in harder.

"You ate your salad fast enough."

"I am not to be trifled with."

"And you think I am?" he asked, leaning in, his breath hot on her neck. "I am a monster," he said, keeping his words so soft no one else could hear them. It would look to anyone else like lovers lost in conversation. "I drove my own mother out of the palace with my behavior. Do you truly want to test me? You have nowhere to run."

He moved away from her, straightening in his chair and flashing a charming smile. "Clearly you were very hungry, *agape*," he said, drawing attention to her empty plate.

Everyone looked at her and she looked down at her plate. "I ate it so quickly you'd think I'd just… dumped it into a potted plant," she said.

"We can pass on your compliments to the chef," Tabitha said, clearly trying to smooth things over and make it so everyone wasn't staring at her.

Tabitha was blessed with social graces that Zara would never have. Even if she tried. And right now she was very determined not to try.

A war was declared between herself and Andres. A quiet, determined war. One she had a feeling could get quite messy.

"Thank you," Zara said.

"You will enjoy dessert, I think," Kairos said. "We'll serve it after my speech."

"Excellent," Zara said, smiling widely while mentally calculating her next move.

The plates were cleared and Zara's stomach growled. Andres would pay for that.

Kairos stood, and so did Tabitha. They both made their way to the front of the room, and as they did, the rest of the room stood too. Some sort of sign of respect, she imagined. She followed suit, but as she did, Andres took hold of her arm and started to lead her away from the table.

"What are you doing?" she asked.

He didn't respond; he only led her through the crowd, using them as a shield to make their exodus less conspicuous.

They slipped through a side door in the ballroom and out into the corridor, and he pushed her back into the alcove they'd been in before, pressing her back against the wall.

"Do not test me," he said, his voice low, hard.

"Why not?" she asked. "You are intent on testing me."

"But I am the one with the power, little one, and you are not."

Zara didn't think about her next move until it was too late. Fueled by anger, by frustration, she allowed herself to be led by instinct. She reached down, cupping the most vulnerable part of Andres's body. "Is that so? Then perhaps I should find ways to seize some of my own control."

Her pulse thundered in her ears, blood roaring through her veins like a beast. Rage, and something else on the heels of it that she couldn't readily name. Something that made her shake. Made her ache.

"Is that a threat or a promise?" he asked, his voice deeper suddenly, huskier.

She leaned in, her teeth scraping his neck. "Both."

He held her tightly, keeping her close, his dark

gaze intense on hers, his grip like iron. "You bit me, you little monster."

"Your concerns were not unfounded. I may bite you again, and rest assured, unlike yours, my threats are not empty."

"I do hope that your current threat isn't empty." He rolled his hips forward slightly, emphasizing just what threat he meant.

Heat flooded her face, but she didn't release her hold on him. She would not allow him to see that she was affected. She was issuing a threat to his person; she was not touching him for the sake of a thrill.

Still, she became incredibly conscious of the heat of his body. Of the fact that he was growing hard beneath her touch.

How was that possible? How could he possibly be aroused by this?

She realized her breaths had grown shorter, faster, that she ached in places that had never been touched by another person. That she was aroused, as well. And that, more than anything, made her want to squeeze down on him. To hurt him. To make him sorry for putting either of them in this position. She didn't want to be here. Didn't want to be stuck in the palace, engaged to a man she didn't know. Trapped in another life that wasn't of her choosing.

She found herself tightening her fingers around

his arousal. She looked down, caught the glitter of her engagement ring on the hand that was squeezing him. Then she looked back up at his face. A mistake.

She barely had a chance to register the hot, angry glitter in his dark eyes before he closed the distance between them, his mouth crashing down onto hers.

The force of him pushing her back against the wall shifted her hand, her palm sliding over his hardness before coming to rest on his flat stomach, crushed between their bodies as he angled his head and slipped his tongue between her lips.

He proved then what he'd said before. He had the power. She could do nothing, not in this moment. Nothing but simply surrender to the heat coursing through her, to the electrical current crackling over her skin with a kind of intensity she'd never even imagined existed.

His hands were firm and sure on her hips, his body pinning her to the wall as he sought restitution for her attempt at claiming control.

He shifted, grabbing hold of her wrists, freeing her trapped hands for just a moment before lifting them, pinning them back against the wall and pressing his body more completely against hers. "You want a fight?" He growled the words against her mouth. "I can give you a fight, Princess. We don't have to do this the easy way." He angled his head, parting his lips from hers, kissing her neck. She shivered, fear and arousal warring for pride of place inside her. "But if you want to test me, you have to be prepared for the results. I do not know what manner of man you have been exposed to in the past, but I am not one that can be easily manipulated."

He rocked his hips against hers, showing her full evidence of the effect she was having on his body. She should be angry, disgusted. Instead, she felt all the more powerful. She hadn't hurt him, but she had succeeded in making him react. She not only enraged him; she turned him on. She had spent so much of her life being ignored that eliciting such a powerful response from such a man gratified her in ways she never could have anticipated.

She didn't know a kiss could be so many different things. That it could serve so many purposes. That it could make her feel hot, cold, afraid, enraptured. But it did. It was everything, and nothing she should ever have allowed to happen between them.

But it had happened. And it was too late to stop it. She wasn't even sure she wanted to stop it.

Her heart was thundering so hard she was afraid it might crack through her chest, before attempting to beat straight through his.

She was furious. With him, with this. She

wanted to punish him. Wanted to make him pay. For making her feel helpless. Even when she had been captive in the palace in Tirimia, she thought there was hope. But here, she wasn't kept in bondage and chains, wasn't made to stay put with threats. Here, she was simply stripped of options. Shown how small she was in the vast context of the palace, of a country she didn't know. She couldn't go back to her own country, and Andres knew that. Couldn't return to the only home she knew for fear of the safety of her protectors.

He had made her famous now. Putting a ring on her finger and parading her in front of all those people. Had stolen her anonymity. And beyond that, she had no money, no clothes beyond the far too formal princess wardrobe that had been procured for her upon arrival in Petras.

She wanted him to understand that helplessness. To feel it too.

If he was going to take her choices from her, then she would make certain he felt the weight of that. She would be a millstone around his neck. His punishment.

She flexed her hips against his, pushing back, changing the angle of her head and leaning in, claiming his mouth with her own before biting his lower lip. He growled, pressing her hands more firmly against the wall, deepening the kiss, consuming her as if she were the dessert they were missing in the ballroom.

She had spent very little time imagining what it would be like to be kissed. She had craved kind smiles and closeness more than anything physical. But she had thought about it a small amount. And when she had, it had been gauzy. Soft. She had imagined slow, gentle touching. Something sweet and slow-building. She had expected to feel a kiss only on her lips.

She had not expected this explosion. Had not expected a knot of emotion and need that she couldn't even begin to untangle. Had not expected to feel the kiss in every part of herself, over her skin, beneath it, in the deepest, most secret parts of herself.

But he was too protected. And this was nothing new for him. He was a self-confessed playboy who practiced no decency or restraint; he had told her himself. He was shielded by that. By his experience. By his perfectly tailored suit that kept him separate from her.

Without thinking, she reached out, tearing at his tie, loosening the knot. His mouth was still fused to hers, his tongue sliding in deep, tasting her, tormenting her. She couldn't separate out her feelings anymore. Couldn't work out what was arousal, what was rage. It had all grown into a ball of intensity in her chest that was threatening to burst from her if she didn't do something. If she didn't find a release for it.

She was being driven by something else entirely now. There were no thoughts. There was no strategy. She gripped the sides of his shirt, tugging it open, buttons popping off and scattering onto the floor. She put her hand on his chest, gratified when he pulled away, air hissing through his teeth. Yes, she was getting to him. She had affected him. She had broken through the wall. They were in a fight. A fight for control. And beneath that, a fight for something else entirely.

Rough hair covered hot skin, the sensation beneath her fingertips foreign, enticing. Beneath that, he was hard. She looked down, admiring the definition of his muscles. He was a man. So very different from her. She had spent a great deal of her life around men, but she had never experienced a man on this level. Had never truly appreciated what it meant that men were different from women. She appreciated it now.

He released his hold on her, cupping her chin, holding her face steady, keeping his eyes on hers as he reached between them, his hand on his belt buckle. He started to work the fine leather through the silver clasp, before undoing the button on his pants. All the while watching her face. She knew he was checking to see if she was frightened. To see if she wanted him to stop. She didn't know if she did. She had a vague idea of what they were headed toward. Of what was coming next. Nothing about it frightened her. Nothing about it made her want to say no.

He let go of her chin, putting both hands on her hips, slowly gathering her skirt, drawing it upward, exposing her legs. He moved one hand between her thighs, his touch a sharp, unexpected shock. His fingertips slipped slowly beneath the edge of her underwear, a feeling of white-hot pleasure streaking through her as he rubbed the bundle of nerves there. She was slick, and he used it to great effect, creating a ripple of pleasure that threatened to overtake her.

This wasn't a struggle anymore. This was a surrender.

She couldn't even regret that. Couldn't even spare a moment to be angry.

He kept his eyes on hers as he touched her, as he stole her breath and pushed her closer toward heights she hadn't known existed. He was touching her. He saw her. In that moment, they weren't warring. They were connected.

She didn't feel afraid that she was so close to another person. That she felt as if she needed him. As if he mattered.

He tugged her panties to the side, pressing his pelvis against hers, the heat of his bare arousal shocking, exhilarating.

He flexed his hips, the blunt head of him pushing up against the slick entrance to her body. She wondered, just for a moment if she should fear this. She didn't. She couldn't. She wanted him closer. Wanted to capture this one moment of fighting on the same side as him. Of pursuing the same goal. Of being connected to another person in a way she had never been.

This moment of not being alone.

He thrust upward, a sharp, shocking pain lancing her as he did. A shocked cry escaped her lips, swallowed up by his harsh groan. He buried his face in her neck, withdrew slightly from her body before pushing in deep again. She gasped, biting her lower lip, squeezing her eyes shut tight, trying to keep tears from falling as the tearing sensation receded.

He wrapped one arm around her waist, holding her steady as he began to move inside her. The pain faded into the background, replaced by a strange feeling of being claimed, invaded. Filled. But with that was a sense of security, of being a part of another person in the way she never had been before.

He filled her, and as he did, he filled that void in her chest that had been there since she was a girl, taken from the only home she'd ever known. Alone in the world.

She wasn't alone now.

He found his rhythm, and as he did, she found hers. Not fighting against him, but moving with him. Not the same as he did, but to complement. Their differences fit here. Her softness working with his hardness. Her body yielding as his advanced. And she learned quickly that surrendering here gave her power that she'd never imagined she possessed.

He kissed her, rocking hard against her body. She barely had time to grab hold of his shoulders before she was sent straight over the edge into oblivion. Left spent, shaking and dependent on him to keep her from sliding onto the floor.

Wave after wave of sensation she was unprepared for. She had no defenses against it, because she'd never seen it coming.

She'd had no idea it would be like this. None at all.

As he growled out his own release, his body pinning hers harder to the wall, she wrapped her arm around his head, holding him steady, her fingers laced through his hair. He stayed there for a moment, breathing hard before wrenching himself away from her. Leaving her cold, empty.

And no less connected to him.

That should have eased, shouldn't it? Now that he wasn't inside her, shouldn't she feel the change?

She looked up into his eyes, dark, blank. And

she knew that for him it was over. She knew that no part of her lingered inside him, as he did her.

And then, as if to prove her suspicion, he turned on his heel and walked away, leaving her standing there against the wall shivering and changed.

CHAPTER SEVEN

ANDRES CALLED HIMSELF ten kinds of fool on his way back to his chamber. He couldn't go back into the luncheon, not after that. Anyway, Zara had destroyed his shirt.

He had left her there, similarly destroyed. Altered.

But he didn't fix things, he only broke them further, so there had been no point in him staying. He hadn't been able to.

He hated isolation. Hated it. But it was the only way he could regain control after something like that. A fact driven into him from childhood.

It was why his mother had always locked him in his room after an outburst. Why he was condemned to staying in the palace when the royal family went out.

Now he was doing the same to himself. Because he had to do something, anything, to calm the raging monster inside him that had claimed control of his actions.

An image flashed through his mind, her hands wrapped around the fabric, tugging hard, sending the buttons onto the marble floor. The look in her eyes, dark, determined. As with all things she had been uncivilized, untutored, and wholly authentic.

For a man who had no idea what his own personal authenticity might look like, it was alarming.

But that wasn't what disturbed him now. Wasn't what caused rage to roar through his veins like a ravening beast.

He had lost control.

Civilizing Zara was one thing. It was himself… that was where he failed. He was cracking apart inside. The years spent forming himself into the man he was seemingly washed away on the tide of lust Zara had inspired in him.

The woman was new. The failure was not.

His best effort had never been good enough. When he was a boy he had been the one at the formally set table dropping silverware, fidgeting in his seat. Crawling underneath the table to pick up a crouton he had dropped. And when the thought to get up struck him, he had never been able to control the impulse. Sometimes he would think of something to say, and it would just spill out of his mouth. His father would simply glare at him, his eyes ice. Kairos would pretend it wasn't happening.

His mother would cry. As though he had done it to her personally. As though he had done it to hurt her.

She had felt everything so deeply. He would make a loud sound and the poor woman would tremble. He wondered at that now, though he'd never understood it then.

Finally, they had stopped allowing him to attend events. The solitude had been frustrating, but better than being set up to fail. Every luncheon, every church service, ever concert…it all seemed designed to doom him.

Then the last Christmas banquet had come. The last one his mother had been at.

He had destroyed that too.

He had tried, and it hadn't been good enough. He had made her cry one too many times. And he was certain that his father, that Kairos imagined it had been like every other time before. But Andres had felt it. When his mother had wiped that final tear off her cheek, he knew that it would be the last year she ever cried for him.

Of course, in order for him to stop making her cry, she couldn't see him anymore.

None of them saw her again. Because of him.

Kairos never blamed him, because Kairos was too honorable to ever think about doing such a thing. Kairos only blamed him for the loss of his fiancée when it suited him, and then, never as much as Andres felt he deserved. Given that, he would never, ever blame him for their mother leaving.

Their father had. Angrily. Loudly. And Andres hadn't even been able to feel sorry for himself because it had been true. He had known it then; he knew it now. *You will never amount to anything. You're nothing but a disappointment. If that was your best, if that was you trying, then you will never, ever succeed.*

He had known it to be true then, and so he had simply gone off to do what he wanted. He hated trying to conform to palace life anyway. Who did he have left to please? His father believed him to be beyond redemption, his mother was gone. Kairos cared, if only in a long-suffering way, and didn't seem to mind what Andres did as long as it didn't affect him.

His indiscretion with Francesca had not been acceptable as far as Kairos was concerned, but then, Andres was not terribly surprised by that.

It was because of that that he was trying. Because of Kairos. Because if nothing else his brother had always cared for him, in spite of the fact that he had been nothing but trouble. Nothing but a disappointment. He was trying, and Zara was intent on seeing him fail.

That was why he had dragged her out of the ballroom. That was why he had allowed her to push him into this power struggle. Allowed her to push him into trying to one-up her.

And then she had grabbed him. She had meant it to be a threat, and he was not naive enough to think she wouldn't follow through with it. Zara was a survivor. A fighter. He would not underestimate her. Had not underestimated her from the moment he had walked in and seen her in his bedroom.

He had anticipated that she would be difficult. That dealing with the engagement, the upcoming marriage, wouldn't be an easy thing. He had never anticipated he would lose his mind completely and take her up against a wall in the palace. In public, where anyone could have found them. Yes, they were in a slightly hidden alcove, but all it would have taken was someone to wander out of the banquet and get lost looking for the restroom.

That was not how a prince was to treat his future princess. It was certainly nothing Kairos would ever have done with Tabitha. Of course, his brother was the authority on unhappy marriages. That was becoming more and more apparent.

That was also Andres's fault.

His actions had forced Kairos into the speedy marriage in the first place.

The reason he had to atone now.

And Zara was making things impossible for no reason other than her own bloody-mindedness. She had nowhere else to go. He didn't treat her badly.

What happened back there wasn't treating her badly?

He gritted his teeth, shoving the thought down

deep. Trying to ignore the growing unease in his chest.

He threw open the doors to his bedchamber before slamming them behind him. He pushed his fingers through his hair, and only then did he realize that his hands were shaking. How could he have done such a thing? How could he have allowed her to push his control like that?

How could he allow her to prove that he was still nothing more than the boy he'd been? The boy who couldn't sit still for more than a couple of minutes. Who couldn't fight any impulse that came upon him. He had wanted her, and so he had taken her.

Without a condom.

He swore, taking his suit jacket off and casting it onto the floor. He had never in his life forgone the use of protection. In truth, he was quite controlled in his debauchery. He didn't keep himself from doing anything he wanted, but if he wanted to resist something, he was able. Sure, he didn't have to exercise self-denial very often, but he was capable of it. Was capable of making responsible decisions.

Not today.

In public. In the middle of the day. Without protection.

The door burst open behind him and he whirled around to see Zara standing there, her hands clenched at her sides, her expression stormy, her dark eyes glistening. Her glossy black hair, which had been expertly schooled into a bun earlier, was disheveled now, all but shouting about what had taken place only moments earlier.

"How dare you walk away from me?" Her voice was quivering with indignation.

There was no doubt that Zara's feathers were thoroughly ruffled. Though he had a feeling there was nothing he could do at this point to unruffle them. In truth, she had been rather ruffled from the first moment he saw her. It was the effect he seemed to have on her.

That didn't bother him. What disturbed him was the effect she seemed to have on him.

"Did you want me to stay and initiate another round? We were standing in the hallway. Anyone could have walked by," he said, throwing the same accusations at her that he had just thrown at himself.

"That didn't bother you before."

No, it didn't. Because he hadn't been thinking. He hadn't been in control.

He ground his teeth together, his heart thundering hard. He was...angry. At his body, for betraying him as it always did. At himself, for his weakness.

At her, for making him vulnerable.

Before he knew what he was doing, he growled,

crossing the room toward her. Her eyes widened, and she shrank back from him, her back hitting the wall.

"You think the wall will save you? I think we've proven that it won't," he said, rage making him reckless. Making him cruel.

He wanted to use his words to drive a wedge between them. To push her away. He didn't want her to look at him with desire.

"You are not touching me again until you explain yourself."

"What's to explain? I wanted you. I had you." With no control, no finesse, no care for anything at all. He hadn't even asked her if she wanted it. Yes, her body language had given every indication that she did, but he hadn't even known how innocent Zara was. He still wasn't entirely certain. She had acted boldly back there, but that meant nothing. He was afraid to ask. Now that it was too late, he was very afraid indeed.

"And then you left."

"Again, Princess, what did you want from me?"

"I thought we might go back in for dessert," she said, her voice wobbling.

That innocence, the insecurity, tore at him like claws and yet he could not stop himself from putting more distance between them.

He laughed, the sound carrying no humor. "So you thought I would go back in there with no buttons on my shirt? After all, a little *creature* pulled them off."

She is not the creature. You are the monster.

Her expression turned all the more stormy. "I am not a creature. I am a woman. As I think I just proved." She was as haughty as ever. As prideful. Her chin tilted upward, her eyes full of determination.

But she was also vulnerable. He could see it there, written on her face plainly. And there was nothing he could do about it. He was not the man to handle vulnerable women.

If his history was any indicator, he was the man who chased vulnerable women away.

"And I am a man," he said, keeping his tone dry. "So there is nothing all that exceptional about attraction exploding between us."

She frowned. "Even though we were fighting?"

"Especially because we were fighting," he said, his voice rough.

"That makes no sense to me."

"Then I question the sort of lovers you've had in the past."

It was her turn to laugh. "I've had no other lovers."

It was the answer he had been afraid of. The rage in his blood turned to ice, settling in the pit of his stomach. "Is that so?"

"Of course I haven't. I had never even kissed a man before you."

Mother of God. Had she even known what was exploding between them out there in the hall? Had she even realized where it might go? What had he done?

In that moment he despised himself. He hadn't thought it was possible for him to reach a new depth of hating his own lack of self-control. The loss of his mother, what happened with Francesca, he had imagined that was the worst of it. Right now, looking at this angry, confused woman who had been a virgin only minutes earlier, he realized there were entirely new depths he hadn't even known about.

"How is it you have survived this long?" he growled, aware that he was allowing his anger at himself to spill out and hit the wrong target. "You are so naive it is painful. By rights you should have been devoured by a wolf in the forest."

Her eyes were filled with righteous indignation. "I feel as though I *was* just devoured by a wolf."

"If I had devoured you, little one, you would hardly be standing here radiating rage."

"Perhaps, had you not run away from me like a scared little boy, I would not be standing here radiating rage."

For a moment, he saw himself as exactly that.

A scared little boy failing at his duty yet again. Going off into isolation.

No.

He slammed his hand against the wall, right by her head. "Were I a little boy you would not behave so satisfied as you apparently were."

"You can't minimize and maximize the impact of what happened in the same argument," she said, her eyes never wavering from his.

"I can do whatever I like." He pushed away from her, his heart raging. "I am the prince here."

She rolled her eyes, having the gall to look bored. "And I am a princess."

"Princess of the caravans," he said. "Very compelling. You would be nothing here in my country were it not for your engagement to me. An engagement that you seem intent on preventing when you know it's the only way you'll ever make anything of yourself. You want to know who you really are? Apart from me? Impoverished. Would you like to explore the meaning of that? Being cold, being hungry, being truly alone."

The color drained from her face and he felt an answering ache expanding in his stomach. He didn't think it was possible to be any more of a bastard than he already was. Yet again, he was proved wrong.

"Whatever freedom you imagine you might find in that," he continued, "I guarantee it will not be there. Here? With me? I will give you money, power, access to education, a chance to make a difference. Not sleeping in the street, which I feel you may also think an advantage."

She was now completely white-faced and still, like a small marble statue, turned to stone by his words.

"My mistake," he said. "You were imagining that you might have a life if you left me, and I have just stolen your illusion. What were you thinking? That I might finance your life without the benefit of having you in my bed?"

"No." Furious color rose in her cheeks. "Of course I didn't think that. I thought that I could… perhaps find out what I wanted to do…"

"For work? You have no job experience. You have no life experience. Forgive me, Princess, but you need to understand that growing up in the wilderness, surrounded by a band of people lost somewhere in the last century, does not give you the necessary tools to exist inside an urban society."

"I am not naive, nor am I stupid. The screaming in the palace… Andres, you would pray to God to have those memories removed from your head. However, it doesn't work that way. If I had any innocence left, it all was lost then. So do not treat me as though I am some kind of wide-eyed child. I stopped being a child when I was six years old." She took a deep breath. "I am the only survivor of a terrible attack on the royal family. I was whisked out of my bedroom in the dead of night by my mother's maid, screams filling the air behind us, screams that echo in my head even now. Screams that most certainly belonged to my mother, my father. My brother. I am left with nothing but the sounds and my imagination to weave every dark image with them. I do not know exactly how they died, but I have thought of countless ways. Dreamed the most nightmarish things. Do not mistake me for an innocent."

Her words felt like a crushing blow against his chest. He wondered, for some reason, if anyone had ever taken care of her. Yes, the people who had raised her had certainly seen to her needs. Her basic needs. But he wondered if anyone had truly cared for her.

His mother had left, and his father had been distinctly disinterested, but he'd had servants, nannies who at least approximated some kind of love. Who had read him stories, and tucked him in. Had anyone read her stories? She was a girl, a girl who had thick, luxurious hair. Surely someone would have needed to braid it for her? Had anyone ever done so? It seemed a crime if no one had.

As if you've treated her any better. You were rough. You took no care for her virginity. And you must've known. There's no way you couldn't have.

He had only contributed to her loneliness. He had left her. He hadn't taken care of her. He had been so focused on her failing him that he hadn't taken into account the fact that he had failed her.

Just as he had failed his mother. His father. His brother.

He had a chance to endeavor to do better by her. At least now.

"Go into the bathroom," he said, unable to modify his tone.

She stayed rooted to the spot, glaring at him intensely.

"Must you be stubborn about everything?" he asked. "Go into the bathroom."

She practically snarled as she pushed away from the wall and stomped past him, heading into the bathroom.

He followed, undoing the last of the buttons on his shirt before casting it, and his jacket, down onto the ground. He tried to fight the heat that was pouring through his veins. This was not the time. He slowly undid his belt buckle, the button on his pants, and left both of them behind as he continued on. By the time he entered, he was naked.

Zara looked up at him, eyes wide. "What are you doing?"

He bent down, turning the handle on the bathtub. "I am giving you a bath. I'm certain that you feel in need of one."

She crossed her arms over her chest as though she was trying to protect herself and looked away. "I do."

"Then, take your dress off."

She shrank in on herself, her expression suspicious. "I don't know that I'm ready to be naked with you."

"It's a bit late for that."

She locked her attention on to him, a blush coloring her cheeks. "It is not too late. We weren't naked."

"No, but I was just inside you."

The color in her cheeks intensified. "Well, I don't know if I'm ready for that to happen again."

She was so raw. So hurt. He was the lowest creature. This was too little, too late, and he knew it.

"I left you so I wouldn't hurt you," he said. "And...and because it was the only way I knew to get control over myself."

She looked up at him. "What?"

"I was rough with you. I was...beyond myself. It is something of a default. A...a punishment for me to remove myself from people when I...misbehave."

She frowned. "You punish yourself?"

"When I need it."

"Oh."

He let out a sharp breath. "I swear to you, I will not touch you like that. Not now. Not until you say." A skeptical light glistened in her dark brown eyes. "I only want to take care of you." Were she another woman, one who did not deal in uncomfortable honesty, she would not have believed him. If she were another woman, and this were another time, he would not have believed himself.

"Turn around," she said.

He obeyed, and he heard rustling behind him. He was hard again. And he despised himself for that too. He had good intentions. Sadly his body did not. His body did not understand how to keep its word.

But he would. He would overcome. He would prove himself now, though he had failed his earlier tests. He did have control over himself now. Yes, he had spent a great many years not exercising that control, but he knew it was there.

He would prove it now. This was the ultimate atonement. The ultimate test.

He heard the sound of her disturbing the water, and he closed his eyes, trying very hard not to imagine what it would look like as she sank down into the tub. Trying very hard not to imagine what her bare skin would look like.

He had shown restraint that first day, when he plucked her out of the bath and threw her onto his bed. He had not given himself permission to look at all of her bare, silken skin. He would not show such restraint today. Today, he would look.

He would not touch her, not until she begged for him to, but he would look.

He waited a moment, then without waiting for her permission turned. She was submerged beneath the water, only the tops of her shoulders and her head visible above the surface.

Andres walked toward the tub, stepping into it, sinking down across from her. The water level rose, and her eyes widened. "A bit late to play the blushing virgin. You should have affected that bit earlier."

"I'm still practically a virgin."

He laughed, but the sound carried no humor. "Not even a little bit, *agape*."

He reached out, wrapping his arm around her waist and turning her so that she was facing away from him, wedged between his legs. She squeaked as he adjusted their positions, but she didn't fight him. "Well, it isn't as though I have a vast array of experience."

She was determined to fight him. Every step of the way. If he didn't enjoy it so much, it might irritate him.

"You don't want a vast array of experience," he said, softening his tone. "You said yourself you are not prepared for any more."

She shifted, the round curve of her butt brushing against his arousal. "I said not right *then*."

"You are the most difficult creature."

She turned to look over her shoulder. "So are you. You are so determined to have your way."

He lifted his hand out of the water and caught her chin. "This is not about having my way. I am trying. For my brother, for my country. You have not been honest with me."

"What do you mean?"

"You told me you had accepted this."

"I never said that."

"Scoot forward, and lay your head back."

"Why?"

"Why do you insist on arguing with everything I say?"

She had no response to that. Instead, she complied. He held her tightly as she lowered her head backward, her dark hair slipping beneath the water, fanning out around her. His eyes were drawn to the pale, rounded curves of her breasts, visible just above the surface of the water. In fact, the new pose brought all of her body much closer to the surface, revealing each curve, dip and hollow. But he had promised he wouldn't touch. Not in that way. So he didn't. Instead, he helped her tip her head back farther, careful to keep the water out of her face.

Once her hair was wet, he guided her back up between his thighs, reaching for one of the cut-glass bottles that was resting on the edge of the tub. He tipped it to the side, putting a bit in his hand before replacing it, and turned his focus back to her. He buried his fingers in the dark, silky locks.

"What are you doing?"

"Washing your hair."

He felt her shoulders go rigid. "Why?"

"You are far too full of questions."

"And you are full of questionable behavior."

"Has anyone ever taken care of you, Zara?"

He felt her frame shrink. "I never wanted for food. Or shelter. I was quite adequately taken care of."

"No. That isn't what I meant. Who cared for you? Did anyone do anything beyond simply ensuring that you would not die?"

"What else is there?"

He continued working the shampoo through her hair. "There is this."

"Clean hair won't keep me alive." She sounded subdued now, even though she was still challenging him.

"Is being kept alive enough?" He did not let the question go deep enough that he might be tempted to answer it himself. For himself.

"It has served me well so far."

"But you want more. Which is why you are pushing back so hard on the engagement."

"Or perhaps I simply don't like you. Maybe it isn't the marriage. Maybe it's you."

He leaned in, scraping his teeth over the top of her shoulder. "You like me well enough. At least, in the most important way I can think of where marriage is concerned."

He felt her shiver beneath his touch. "Sex isn't everything."

"Says the near virgin. Sex is quite a few things. Sex is a wonderful source of release. A way to make yourself feel close with someone when you aren't truly close with anyone. And a wonderful way to destroy relationships and family ties." This last part came out more bitter than he'd intended.

"You speak from experience."

"Far too much experience."

"I am curious, Andres." She slithered out of his hold, turning and backing up against the opposite side of the tub. "Why did you do it? Why did you sleep with Kairos's fiancée when you could have had any woman you wanted?" She tilted her head to the side. "Did you love her?"

"No," he said, "I did not love her. I did not even know her, or like her especially."

"Then why would you do it?"

His throat grew tighter, and he couldn't possibly say why. He didn't think he could answer her question either, since it was one he had asked himself many times over the past five years. Except now, for some reason, when the question came from her instead of from himself, he felt an answer rising to the surface. "Alcohol, mainly. As I told you, I didn't even remember what had happened the next morning."

"That isn't all."

It wasn't.

He swallowed and took a deep breath. "Kairos was the only relationship I had yet to damage. I kept waiting for the other shoe to drop. Kept waiting for him to disown me for some antic or another. And he never did. It was hell waiting. Like the blade to the guillotine was hovering above my neck and I knew it would drop, just not when. I decided to drop it myself."

"But… It didn't work. He didn't disown you."

His throat grew even tighter. "No." He had tested Kairos, badly, and Kairos had proved to be the stronger man, the superior man as always. He had proved that Andres was weak. "No, he did not. Just another reason I am honor-bound to comply with him now. Why I must do this for him. I faltered. He did not."

Suddenly, Zara sank beneath the surface of the water, submerging her head completely. When she rose again, she came up slowly out of the water, lifting her arms and sluicing the water droplets from her face, brushing her hair back. The action revealed her breasts. Plump, round, dark, rosy nipples that were more beautiful than he could ever have imagined. She settled again, hiding her body from his view. Then she began to move toward him.

Her dark eyes were locked with his, her expression questioning. She reached out, touching his cheek with her palm. She said nothing; she only leaned forward, pressing her lips firmly against his. When they parted, she was still looking at him. Looking far too deeply for his liking, as though she could see down deep inside him. Down to places not even he ever looked.

"Did it make you less lonely? Being with her?" she asked, her tone serious.

"No," he said. "I felt nothing after being with her."

"You said…it was about control, but… Is that another reason why you left me out there? Because you felt nothing after?"

How could he explain he left her for the opposite reason? That he left her because he felt too much. Because it felt as though she had reached into his chest and ground broken glass into his heart?

"No, that isn't why," he answered, his voice rough.

"I only ask a lot of questions because you make me." She arched a dark eyebrow, letting her fingertips trail down the line of his jaw, down his neck, where she pressed her palm flat against his chest. "Just think how much faster all this would go if you were direct with me. That's how we do things in the forest."

"Do you also collect berries, live in burrows and bunk with squirrels?"

"Don't be mean." She leaned in and bit him on the chin. "I did not live with squirrels."

He gripped her chin with his thumb and forefinger. "I feel quite a lot when I'm with you. I left because I lost control. That never should have happened. You were a virgin. You could not have known how far I was going to take it. It was wrong of me."

"I knew. I'm not completely ignorant. That's one thing about living in such close quarters with other people. You are forced to share some intimacies. You simply accept that certain things will happen around you and you are obliged to look the other way. As a result, I have been well exposed to certain facts of human life."

"Being exposed to and experiencing are two different things."

"Stop treating me like I'm a child. Or a creature. I am a woman. And though I have been able to make few decisions about my own life, I do know my mind."

"I know that."

She tilted her head to the side. "Do you feel guilty?"

"I just said that I did."

"No, I mean about the engagement. Our marriage."

"There is no other option. There is no point entertaining guilt over it."

She moved her hand farther down his chest, her eyes never leaving his. "I have a feeling you don't have any room inside you for more guilt."

Cursed woman. Why did she have to see things so clearly? "Are you charging for this session?"

"What does that mean?"

"Like a therapist. They charge per hour to listen to you talk about your feelings."

"That seems like a waste of money to me. You could go out into the woods and just scream until you feel better."

He looked down at her bland expression. "Is that what you do?"

"I have."

He cupped her face with his hands. "What makes you scream, Zara?"

"The first time I did it," she said, looking down for a moment, "it was after my parents died. I ran into the woods. And I knew I was alone. Really, really alone. So it didn't matter if I screamed. I had to behave myself at the palace. I had to be a princess. But out there, I didn't have to be anything. Nothing but sad. Nothing but lonely. So I howled like a wolf. I don't know for how long. No one heard me, or if they did no one came for me. When I went back…"

"Did you feel better?"

"Not really. But I could breathe." She traced the path of a water droplet over his chest. "So whenever I had trouble breathing, that's what I would do. I was alone a lot. I found ways to make it bearable. Ways that it was an advantage."

He had a flash of his own life. His own behavior. Parties. Drunkenness. Sleeping around with any woman who happened to show interest. That was how he combatted the years of isolation as a child.

An isolation that had been an illusion. Locked in a bedroom, in a palace full of people, you could never scream.

So he had found new ways to learn to breathe.

"Perhaps you could take me to your mountain someday and show me," he said.

"Are you lonely right now?" she asked.

"No," he said, and he found that it was the truth.

"I'm not lonely either." She pressed her mouth to his, light, tentative. "You can touch me now. I'm ready."

He didn't deserve such easy forgiveness, but he would be damned if he didn't take it.

He did not need to be asked again. He claimed her mouth, his touch anything but tentative. She said she was ready. Giving him permission showed that she knew what she wanted. And he would take her at her word, because he had no other choice. He had to have her. Had to have this. To chase the full, aching feeling in his chest that was so different from the emptiness that normally lingered there. Yes, this hurt too, but it was a different pain. One that he relished, one that he embraced.

He wrapped his arms around her, her breasts pressed tightly against his chest, slick from the water. He held her tight, tilting her backward so that her hair was in the water again, making sure that he had rinsed all the shampoo away.

He brought her back up, and she wrapped her arms around his neck, her eyes locked on his. There was something in them. Something luminous, filled with wonder. And he knew for a fact that he was undeserving of it.

But he would take it. And he would take her.

He claimed her lips again, delving deep, his tongue sliding against hers. He'd kissed so many women. More than he could count. More than he cared to count. But this was different. As though it were something entirely new. She was not simply another woman; she was Zara. She was wild, spicy, untamed. Like the land she had come from. He tangled his fingers in her newly cleaned hair, holding her hard against him. He was glad that this time they didn't have any clothes between them. But even the water was too much.

He gathered her tightly into him, moving into a standing position, holding her against his chest. He stepped over the edge of the tub, carrying her out of the bathroom and into the bedroom. They were both still wet, but he didn't care. As he had done that first day, he laid her down the middle of the bed, but this time he looked. He looked his fill. From those full breasts, down to her slender waist, the gentle flare of her hips and the dark shadow at the apex of her thighs. Water droplets rolled down her skin and he had a fantasy of licking each and every one of them away.

Already, he was so hard it was painful. She made him shake. Made him feel as if *he* were the virgin. His years, his experience, melted away. Until there was no one else but Zara. Nothing else but this.

She was staring at him, transfixed. "I have never seen a naked man before. Not one... Not one quite like you."

"Meaning?"

"I have occasionally seen men changing. Or getting ready to bathe in the river. I have not seen them aroused."

"And what do you think?"

Color slashed across her high, arrogant cheekbones. Arousal, he thought, not embarrassment. "I very much like it. You. Also it."

He couldn't help laughing at that. "I am glad."

He joined her on the bed, placing his hand on her thigh and drawing it down the length of her leg. He leaned in, pressing a kiss to the inside of her knee. She shivered beneath his touch and he moved forward. He saw a drop of water on her inner thigh and he lapped it up, moving closer to what he craved. He owed her. She had satisfied him out in the hall. And while he knew she had received some pleasure from their coming together, it wasn't enough. She had also been given pain, which meant she deserved a double portion of pleasure. He was her only lover, would be her only lover ever. It was up to him to show her how incredible it could be.

It wasn't entirely altruistic on his part. He craved her. Needed to know what she tasted like. Needed to satiate the hunger that was building inside him for her. That had been from the first moment he saw her. He hadn't realized just how much he wanted her until that moment out in the hall. Until he had lost all control and had had no choice but to claim her.

He took hold of her hips, moving forward and sliding his tongue over her slick flesh, teasing the bundle of nerves he knew was the source of her pleasure. She lifted her rear off the bed, pulling away from him, but he held her fast.

"You can't do that," she said, her voice trembling slightly.

"Of course I can." He ran his tongue over the same path again. "And I intend to do it until you aren't screaming because you're lonely. But because you're screaming my name. You'll scream until you can't breathe because of me."

He lowered his head again, tasting her, satisfying his craving until she was rocking her hips against his mouth, until she was whimpering. He teased the entrance to her body with his finger, sliding it in slowly, before adding a second, establishing a steady rhythm with his lips, tongue and hands. She was close, so close. So wet and ready. And he was so hard he was about to lose all control. But he was intent on giving her this. On satisfying her in this way before he claimed any pleasure for himself.

And then, finally, she screamed her release, her internal muscles tightening around his fingers as she did.

While she was still shivering from the aftershocks, he rose, kissing her lips, positioning himself between her thighs. "Are you ready for me?" he asked, and he prayed to God that she was. Because he had no more restraint left in him.

"I can't," she said, her words breathless.

"Oh, but you can. Don't you know? It's one of the many beautiful, amazing things about being a woman. As many times as I care to pleasure you, you can find release."

She shook her head, closing her eyes tight. "I would never survive it."

"Of course you would. Because I would never let anything happen to you."

Her lashes fluttered, her eyes opening slowly. "Really?"

His chest tightened, unbearably so, the ache rivaling that of the ache in his body. "Yes," he said, his pledge. His vow. And with him, she would not be alone. He would do more than simply keep her alive. He would give her the life she craved.

He swore that only to himself.

"I believe you." She looked at him with such trust, and something quite a lot like panic filled him. How long had it been since someone had trusted him? Kairos might love him, might not have disowned him, but he certainly didn't trust him. Because Andres had not earned his trust. But Zara trusted him. With everything.

He did not deserve it. But he refused to dwell on it. Not now. Not while he was dying to be inside her. Not while his blood was roaring for release.

He tested her, finding her slick and ready. He entered her slowly, inch by agonizing inch, drawing it out to be cautious of her, of her inexperience and any potential soreness. And to torment himself. He deserved a bit of torment for all that he was getting in return.

When he was sheathed to the hilt inside her

body, she gasped, her eyes widening. He found he could not look at her face, for fear he would go over the edge before things even began. He didn't want it to end like that. He wanted to give her more pleasure. Wanted to make sure that he was giving more than he took.

He established a steady rhythm, driving them both toward release. His blood was roaring through his veins like a beast, intent on devouring him whole if it didn't find escape. If it didn't find a way to relieve the intense sensation that was building inside him, so impossibly large he could scarcely breathe around it. Zara arched against him, her breasts pressed into his chest, her hands sliding easily over his back thanks to the water from the tub. She flexed her hips in time with his, instinct more than making up for a lack of experience.

She pushed her fingers through his hair, tugging hard as she claimed his mouth with her own, biting his lower lip before taking the kiss deeper. He moved his hand down her waist, beneath her rear, pulling her up hard against him, drawing her up so that she met each thrust. The tighter he held her, the more she fought to brand the encounter with her own mark. He rolled his hips, his grip on her tight, and she wrenched her mouth from his, angling her face, biting one of the cords of his neck. And he knew, she would have left a physical mark in addition to all the other invisible fingerprints she would leave behind.

Her teeth scraped against his skin as she moved her hand down to his butt, holding him to her as she returned the motion with her hips. That, along with the low, husky growl that vibrated through her being, sent him crashing over the edge before he had a chance to stop himself. Pleasure burst through him like a volcano, the hot flow of his blood almost too much for him to bear. He couldn't breathe. Couldn't think. Could do nothing more than surrender to the overwhelming release.

He reached between them, sliding his thumb over her clitoris. His last thought before there was nothing but the sensations writing through his body was that he needed her to feel this too. Needed her with him in every way. He felt her begin to tremble, and then she arched beneath him, her internal muscles squeezing his arousal tightly, bringing up his own release. Then there was nothing. He buried his head in her neck, kissing her, closing his eyes and letting the world fall away. Until he couldn't remember his own name. Until he couldn't remember himself. A place of bliss.

All too soon, reality rushed back to him. But at least, when he returned to himself he was with Zara.

"Oh," she said, the word coming out on a long breath.

"Are you disappointed?"

"No. I just… I didn't know. I didn't know it could be quite like that."

"Neither did I." And that was true. He had used sex for a great many things in the past. And always, he was in control. If he was seeking numbness, temporary companionship, that was what he would find. A mere distraction, and then he would be diverted for just a while. But he hadn't claimed the control here. This had been a fight to the finish. And right now he could not confidently say he had come out the conqueror.

At the moment, he felt conquered.

"I will have your things moved back into my room." He didn't think the words through before they came out of his mouth, but he meant them. He would reclaim control of the situation. He would have his way. There was no reason for her to sleep in her own bed, not when they had discovered this connection between them.

He hadn't used a condom this time either.

Rather than cursing himself, he felt a kind of grim determination and satisfaction. If she was with child, she wouldn't be able to push back against him about the engagement. About the marriage. And while he had a feeling he had managed to talk some sense into her, insurance didn't hurt.

He ignored the biting guilt that came on the heels of that thought.

"Now you're having me move back in?" she asked.

"That is what I said."

"But you threw me out!"

"And now I am throwing you in. Things have changed."

"The sex, you mean."

"Between men and women there is very little else."

She frowned. "Is that true?

"In my experience. Though what we have is very good sex. As I said, it is not always like that. It has never been like that for me."

"Yes," she said, climbing up the bed, pulling the covers back and burrowing beneath them. "Because you have vast experience." Her voice was muffled by the blankets.

"What are you doing? Are you burrowing?"

"I am not." She shifted beneath the covers. "I'm cold."

"I think you're hiding from me." He pulled the covers back and she made a sharp, short sound of protest. He slipped beneath them, alongside her, and covered them both back up. "Do not hide from me."

He didn't know why he cared. Didn't know why it mattered. Only that he had felt connected to another person for the first time in longer than he could remember, and he didn't want anything to disturb that. He didn't want her hiding from him.

"This is very new."

"I know. You wanted to experience things."

"Well." She shifted, moving away from him slightly. "Now this, and you, are things that I have experienced."

He wrapped his arm around her waist and pulled her up against his body. "This was not a onetime thing. You are going to be my wife. That means you will share my bed."

"If...if I am your wife, and I share your bed, that means you will not share it with other women." It was not a question; her tone was fierce.

He had not intended that. Not at all. But this was a test of his control. He clenched his teeth. "Yes. I swear it."

She looked straight ahead, her dark eyes unreadable. "Then...yes. Yes, we will go forward with the wedding."

CHAPTER EIGHT

ZARA WOKE UP feeling different. It took her a moment to figure out exactly why. Mostly because though she woke up in Andres's room, she woke up in an empty bed. The sheets were cold, and it was clear that Andres hadn't been between them for hours.

She sat up, holding the blankets to her chest. She looked out the small window that was behind the bed, and saw that the sun was high in the clear December sky. She got up, leaving the blankets behind, gazing outside at the landscape. It was covered in snow, the light glittering over the pristine blanket. It was late. She had no idea how late.

They had left the lunch yesterday, and then… all of that had happened. They had come back to the room. There had been the bath. Then the rest. Then more. And eventually, she had fallen asleep. Somewhere in there, she was pretty certain she had agreed to marry him. She looked down at her left hand and saw that she was still wearing his ring. Yes, she had definitely agreed.

And apparently she had also been in bed for nearly twelve hours.

She groaned and turned back to the bed, flopping down over the top of it. Right then the doors to the room burst open. She scrambled for the blankets, pulling them over her naked body.

"Oh, good," Andres said, closing the doors behind him. "You're awake."

"Barely," she said.

"We have somewhere to be."

"What?" She sat up. "Why didn't you tell me?"

"Because I didn't know until recently. And because you have been asleep."

"I would have thought your schedule would be more fixed."

He shook his head. "Regrettably, no. I don't normally live here at the palace."

The statement took her by surprise. She had assumed that Andres lived here. Then she realized she had not been here very long, and they had never discussed it. "You don't?"

"No. I have penthouses in a few of the major cities in the world. I try to avoid being under my brother's roof when possible. Sadly, of late, it has not been possible."

"So we... We won't live here?"

"No. Unless it is very important to you."

She shook her head. "No. I... Which cities?"

"Paris. New York. London."

"I should like to live in those. *All* of them."

"Sometimes we will."

For the first time she felt wholly pleased with the idea of marrying him.

"I see that you like that." A smile curved the corner of his lips. He seemed pleased that she was pleased. And that made her feel...pleased. She had the feeling that sex made people slightly crazy and she was suffering the aftereffects of that. She had spoken very boldly of all she knew about it. Because she had of course been aware that it happened around her in the camp. Caravans, tents, were not soundproof.

Still, she had never had these kinds of feelings about anyone. So the entire concept might as well be foreign.

"I have never been anywhere. Never, not in my life. Coming here to Petras was the first time I had ever been outside Tirimia. And since coming here... I haven't left the palace."

"Well, you will be leaving today."

"I see you have everything all planned out. It would be nice if you would share those plans with me."

"We are going to a Christmas play."

Zara sputtered. That was about the last thing she had expected for him to say. "I didn't expect that."

"Several of the local schools are putting on a program. Kairos and Tabitha were unavailable and someone from the royal family needs to be there."

"So we are going." She was a part of the royal

family now. She was a part of the family. The thought made a warm sensation bloom in her chest and start to spread outward, making her fingertips, her legs, her toes feel warm too. She hadn't realized until that moment just how cold she had been.

"Yes. Your clothes have already been selected and are being sent up."

"If you aren't careful I could fall into the habit of letting you take care of things for me." She took a deep breath. "It's sort of nice not to have to worry about details."

"I'm not worrying about your details. Untold legions of palace staff are. I prefer for them to worry about mine, as well."

"It is quite a luxury."

"I'm surprised to see that you aren't hissing and spitting. I should have used sex to quiet you down from the first moment."

She glared at him, completely annoyed with herself as she felt her face heat. She was certain she was not looking angry so much as flushed and eager. How irritating that being with him had in fact stolen some of her thunder.

"I did not fight with you for no reason. I'm hardly going to do it just for the sake of it."

"Yes, I know, it was all about your freedom."

The warmth in her chest only grew in intensity. She felt…understood. She could not remember the last time, if ever, she had felt that. A knock on the door to the bedchamber broke the tension between them.

"Those would be your clothes. I will leave you to that."

"I'm wrapped in a blanket!"

"Yes, but the stylist is going to dress you anyway. Probably for the best that you are starting out undressed. Saves time."

She lifted a shoulder. "Okay."

"I will meet you downstairs."

Without another word he turned and walked toward the door, opening it for the stylist and leaving her alone with the woman holding a garment bag.

An hour, some makeup and some hair products later, Zara was in the back of a limousine with Andres, driving away from the palace. The roads were clear, but there was snow on either side of them, covering the ground and the pine trees beyond. Little bits of green velvet showing through the pristine blanket of white.

It wasn't so different from the landscape in Tirimia, and yet, as they wound away from the private drive that led to the palace, it started to appear more and more foreign to her. They had driven over the Tirimian border at night when she was brought here to Petras, so she hadn't had a chance to get a sense for the city. Added to that, she had been terrified.

But she was seeing it now. Old churches stood alongside modern high-rises, Georgian-era homes placed near trendy boutiques and bakeries. She was transfixed by the movement. The cars on the road, the people on the sidewalks. It was anything but lonely. Every piece of stone was part of something, touching something else.

She turned to face Andres, suddenly conscious of just how quiet he had been the entire drive. His eyes were on her, assessing. "What are you doing?"

"Watching you."

"I'm not doing anything."

"That isn't true. You're looking at the scenery. Quite prettily, I might add."

A rush of adrenaline and satisfaction filled her. "I don't think I've ever been accused of doing anything prettily before."

"You're very pretty. Everything you do is done prettily as a result."

"Even when I hiss and spit and gnaw on chicken bones?"

"You didn't gnaw the bones."

"I *would* have. If you hadn't dumped my dinner in a potted plant."

He surprised her then by laughing. Not a carefully controlled laugh. Not one designed to mock.

But one filled with humor. "I did dump your dinner in a potted plant, didn't I?"

"Yes. You owe me chicken."

"I will keep that under advisement."

As stunning as the scenery was, she found that she suddenly wanted to keep her eyes on him. He was beautiful when he smiled. His dark eyes glittered in a way they didn't usually, his teeth white against his golden skin. He had a slight dimple on one side of his mouth. One she hadn't noticed before. She had seen him naked, and still, she noticed something new about him. She wondered how long it would take for her to discover every mystery he contained.

Suddenly, she felt panicked, because she was afraid a lifetime might not be sufficient. She was so behind in her learnings on this sort of thing. When it came to the mysteries that passed between men and women, she had to learn to be a princess and a wife, and she had no idea how she would ever accomplish both.

She didn't have time to worry, as just then the limousine pulled up to a large, ornately carved building. "The oldest church in Petras," Andres said, anticipating her question before she spoke it.

"It's beautiful," she said, getting out of the car when the driver opened the door for her.

Andres got out and looped his arm through hers, leading her up the steps. She looked at the

expansive doorway, at the saints and angels fashioned into the stone.

The building was even more spectacular inside.
There was a large basin filled with water, holy
water, she assumed. Beyond that, chairs were set
up facing the stage and a large stained-glass window was positioned above, light filtering through
and casting colors onto the floor below. There
were Christmas trees, large and perfectly dressed,
stationed throughout the sanctuary, lit by white
lights, wrapped in dark red garlands.

As had happened at the palace, the crowd
parted to allow Andres passage.

There was a seat reserved for them in the front,
and once they sat, she sensed all the eyes in the
room on them. At least, until the play began. Children of all ages stood holding candles, singing
songs. The young children didn't sing beautifully,
but they sang loudly. The older children managed
harmonies, their voices echoing beautifully in the
space, filling it, filling her.

When they began the last song, her eyes began
to well up and she grabbed a hold of Andres's
hand, squeezing it tightly, trying to keep tears
from falling. She never cried. She had cried for
her parents. For her brother. Anything after that
hadn't seemed worthy of her tears. But she had
never before cried for beauty. For something so
lovely it seemed it had come from another world.

When the program finished, everyone stood, people milling around the stage and going to speak to the children.

"Can we go tell them how wonderful it was?" she asked Andres.

"If you wish."

"I do."

Zara had always liked children. The clan had been distant with her, but not the children. By the time Zara was an adult, that was her main source of connection. She would spend time leading the children on expeditions through the woods, reading them stories.

Of all the things she had left behind, she missed the children the most.

When they approached, the children looked more awed than excited. But she couldn't blame them. Andres had that effect. "It was a very good performance," Andres said, addressing a small group.

The kids looked down, smiling shyly and scuffing their toes. "Thank you," they said, in an uneven chorus.

Zara hunched down, trying to get on their level. "I enjoyed it very much. You sang so beautifully it made me cry."

A little boy with both front teeth missing looked surprised. "We did? How?"

"Sometimes things can make you cry because

they fill you with so much joy you can't hold it all in. So it leaks out your eyes." At least, she assumed that was why. She didn't have a lot of experience with it.

The boy laughed. "You're funny."

"I know."

She spent the next few minutes talking to the children, while Andres hung back. It was easy for her. Children didn't judge in the same way adults did. Neither did they observe protocol. They didn't keep that reserve to distance that was given to royalty out of respect, because children did not understand respect in the same way adults did. For that she was grateful.

Andres put his hand on her shoulder and she straightened. "It is time for us to leave soon."

"Okay."

As they turned to go, one of the teachers rushed to them. "Prince Andres," she said. "I just wanted to thank you for coming. And this is Princess Zara?"

Zara was astonished that this woman knew her name. But then, she supposed her name might have been mentioned in the media since the luncheon yesterday.

"Yes," Andres said, wrapping his arm around her waist, "my fiancée."

"You are so good with the children, Princess," the woman said.

"I like children," Zara returned.

"Well, if you ever find yourself in need of ways to fill your time, we could always use volunteers in the classroom. People to come and read books, or help with choir."

"I would love to," Zara said. How long had it been since anyone needed her? Since anyone thought she was good at something and wanted to put those skills to use?

It had always been blood. Always been title. This was different, and it was exhilarating. This was being where she belonged, the pieces of herself, scattered on the wind for so many years, finally coming to rest.

Like coming to the end of a long walk in the wilderness, making it to the summit and finally seeing what she'd been traveling toward all her life. Her destiny, laid out before her.

A princess in a palace, with her prince at her side.

"We will put Zara's assistant in touch with you," Andres said.

"I'm Julia Shuler," the woman offered. "If you need to get hold of me."

"Thank you, Julia. I'm looking forward to coordinating something."

"We must go, Princess. We have a reservation."

Zara looked up at Andres. "For what?"

"For that dinner I owe you."

* * *

The restaurant was beautiful, situated at the top of a hill overlooking the glittering city below. Zara had never been to such a fine place, the palace in Tirimia excluded. She had been spoiled by lovely food since coming here, but somehow this felt different. Perhaps because they were making a public showing, together. Perhaps because she had been fashioned into a woman who looked as though she belonged on Andres's arm.

Perhaps just because she was excited. She was out to dinner with Andres. It was, for all intents and purposes, her first date.

She could scarcely think back to the woman she had been yesterday. The one who had tried to sabotage their arrangement by making a spectacle during the luncheon. She felt different now. Being with him had changed something. It had changed her.

She lifted the glass of wine to her lips, trying to orient herself to what was happening. To the fact that she was here. Sitting across from the most handsome man she had ever seen in her life, sipping on the most marvelous drink she'd ever had. She was warm. She was wearing beautiful clothes. There was a teacher who wanted to use her skills.

She was part of the royal family.

"You don't have to volunteer for the schools if

you don't want to," Andres said, taking a sip of his own wine.

"But I want to," she said. "I told you, I want to find out what I'm good at. What I want to do. I was a younger daughter and I imagine that even if I had stayed in Tirimia, this is the sort of thing I would have done. And maybe I can figure out some of the specific needs of the people here if I'm working with them on such a close level. There might be some other things I could arrange. Charities." She smiled. "I enjoyed the kids back in the encampment I lived in. They didn't put so much distance between themselves and me. I really do love children."

"That's good."

She tilted her head to the side. "Why is that good?"

"Because we will have children. We may yet have one on the way already, as careless as we've been."

Her heart stalled, then slammed into her chest. "Oh." Of course. They had taken no precautions against pregnancy. She had not thought of that until now. She waited to feel angry. To feel sad. She didn't. The thought of a baby—Andres's baby—only filled her with more of that same warmth from earlier.

They really would be a family. She had been alone for so long, and now she felt she was spoiled with company. A man who would be her husband, who would share her bed. A child. Just for a moment she allowed herself to be nothing more than completely happy. Filled with joy, filled with anticipation.

"I hope you aren't upset," he said, breaking her out of her reverie.

"Upset? Why would I be upset? I'm…happy."

Andres looked completely shocked by that statement, but there was no way he could have been more surprised than Zara herself. But, surprising as it was, it was true. Today, he had shown her something other than the palace. Today, he had shown her what she could mean, not just to her country, not just to him, but to others. And what others could mean to her. She was beginning to feel that she was part of something. A part of the people here in this country, of the royal family.

"Forgive me for feeling surprised by that, Princess. But just yesterday you tried to get yourself thrown out."

She lifted a shoulder. "Things change."

A shadow fell over his expression, and he took another sip of wine. "I suppose sometimes things do change. But people rarely do."

"Why does that sound ominous?"

"It shouldn't. Just realistic. I want you to understand that just because what you want has changed, it doesn't mean that I will."

"Because you're so very terrible?" She had yet to see evidence of this legendary playboy and lapsed prince. Andres wasn't perfect. She wasn't entirely certain she could characterize him as nice. But she liked him. He was full of passion, fire and intensity. And, though he would deny it, conviction.

Deeper than the conviction was the pain. Pain that she had heard in the cracks of the story he'd told about his mother. In his explanation for why he had slept with his brother's fiancée. How deeply must a man hate himself to try and make everyone else hate him too? Beneath his words now, she sensed it. That same intent.

"There are quite a few people on this earth who would tell you that I am."

"Happily for you, I am not one of them. Which is really quite convenient when you think about it. I doubt you want a wife who hates you."

He laughed, the sound like the edge of a rusty knife's blade. "It may be inevitable. I'm not entirely certain as I've never had a wife before."

"It's only inevitable if you make it so. It's your decision."

"And yours, I think, Princess," he said, a strange kind of insincerity coating his words.

"Then I purpose to like you. For a very long time." She was quite satisfied with the declaration.

"Very kind of you."

A moment later the waitstaff appeared, putting plates down in front of them. It was chicken, which made her smile because he'd remembered that he owed her chicken. "I like you even more now."

"You are very cheaply bought."

"If you recall, I was a gift." She sliced a small piece off her chicken and took a bite. She chewed thoughtfully, then smiled. "I was quite cheap for you. Free even."

"Yes. My little fruit basket."

"On a fruit-basket scale I'm quite large. Impressive."

"Yes, but on the scale of small, feral women, you are tiny."

"I have no frame of reference for playboy princes and how large or small they might be. Though I would consider you large." She felt her face get hot and she took another bite of food.

"Are you trying to engage me in a bit of dirty talk?" His eyes glittered with amusement and she decided that keeping that look on his face would become a goal of hers.

Help children with reading, find useful ways to spend her time, make Andres's eyes glitter.

She added to her list.

"Perhaps. But I have no experience with that."

"Tell me." He shifted in his chair. "What do you have experience with?"

"Well, as you know, I have a great amount of experience wandering the woods alone. As you've seen today, I have some experience with children. I have some experience with grief. And now I have a bit of experience with sex."

The glitter in his eyes turned molten. "Not nearly enough as far as I'm concerned. I will have to expand your education."

"I feel agreeable to that."

"Well, I do live for your agreement."

"In this case, I imagine you might."

A smile curved the corner of his mouth upward. "Do you think?"

"You have quite a bit of power, Andres, and certainly you have some over me. But I don't think I'm wrong in imagining that I might have some over you too."

"Do you not like dessert, Zara?"

"I am fond of cake. Why?"

"You seem intent on ensuring that you never get to have it."

"I do?"

Just then the waiter came back by and Andres stood. "Send my bill to the palace. And we will take a cake."

"Are we leaving?"

"We are. And quickly."

He wrapped his hand around her arm and pulled her up to her feet.

"Why are you in such a hurry?"

"Because," he said, leaning in, "you have tempted me. And now I must have you."

A shiver went down Zara's spine. "You must have me?"

"I *need* you."

How long had it been since anyone needed her? Had anyone ever needed her? She wasn't certain that they had. It felt… It felt good. The ache inside her was changing, shifting. It wasn't a yawning howl of isolation, not that brittle emptiness. This was something else. It was warm, and it burned like fire, creating a desperate feeling at her center that she couldn't quite understand. Desperate to do something. To touch him. To be close to him, skin to skin so that there was no distance between them. To make sure he felt the same thing she did.

He said that he needed her. And she desperately needed that to be true.

Desperately needed to feel connected.

Such a strange thing that, on the heels of feeling that she was in the place she belonged, she realized how much more there was. How much more she wanted.

To not just fit in with this place, but with this man.

The waiter appeared a moment later with a

large bag, containing a white pastry box. Andres accepted it and whispered to her, "This is, I think, having your cake and eating it too."

"I don't understand what that means."

"You're about to."

CHAPTER NINE

ONCE THEY WERE in the limo, they did not head back toward the palace. Rather, they headed deep into the city center. "Where are we going?" Zara asked.

"I have a penthouse near here."

"You left that off your list of residences when we talked about it earlier."

"I like to keep a little mystery."

"Really?"

"No, not really. In fact, there is very little mystery to me. If you take the time to look me up online, you can find out anything you'd ever want to know."

She decided then and there that she didn't need to look him up on the computer. She didn't have any experience using computers anyway, so it wasn't as though she was going to tackle the task in her spare time. But she didn't especially want the outside world's opinion on Andres. She didn't need it. She had her own opinion.

They wove through the evening traffic, down to the city center. The limo driver pulled to the edge of the curb and Andres got out, rounding the back of the car to her side. He opened the door for her and she slid out, accepting his hand as he helped her stand from the vehicle.

"Come on, Princess." For some reason, when he called her that this time it seemed different. Softer, more personal. She held it close to her chest, against the burning embers of warmth that he had stoked earlier.

He led her through the front doors of the building, into the glittering lobby. Shining marble tiles on the floors, rich textured paper on the walls, and grand pillars stationed throughout the space. "This is beautiful."

He tugged on her hand, leading her through quickly, toward the back of the room and the golden elevator doors. "I'll show you around later. Right now I simply intend to show you to my bed."

He whisked her inside the elevator, the doors closing behind them. She leaned back against the wall, her hand on her chest, trying to catch her breath. She could hardly wrap her head around today, around this moment. He wanted her.

He looked at her, frowning slightly. "What?"

She lifted her shoulder. "I just... I did not imagine that I would want this." But she did. She wanted this to be her life. Wanted him to be her life.

"I suppose it has been a bit different than either of us imagined."

"For you too?"

"Well, I never imagined my brother selecting my wife for me. Particularly not one who had been given to the royal family."

"Yes, that was a surprise for both of us."

Her stomach felt as if it dropped about an inch or so as she replayed the words that had just passed between them. What she had said to him. And how he had not returned the sentiment. He had sidestepped. But he had not said that he wanted this too. She was confident that he wanted her, that he wanted her physically, but the rest of it…? She wasn't so certain.

And it mattered. It mattered so very much.

She had learned too much in her time here in Petras. So much that she could scarcely sort it all out. She had learned more about herself than she had imagined there was to learn. She felt too full with it. With this new understanding of emotion. How she could want this man unconditionally, and yet wish strongly that he would fulfill a thousand little conditions she could never begin to list until she felt the lack of them.

One thing was certain, a life of semi-isolation was simpler.

The elevator doors slid open and Andres walked out ahead of her. She followed, emotion still swirling in her chest, in her head. She wondered how things had changed so quickly. How she had gone from simply feeling, simply wanting, to being made of feeling and wanting. The two were different things, she was coming to see.

She followed him out into the hall, her heart thundering heavily. She waited while he unlocked the door, extending his arm, clearly indicating he wanted her to go in first.

She walked past him, into the penthouse. She stopped, turning a full circle in the center of the open-plan living area, trying to orient to her surroundings. She had made a lot of assumptions about Andres based on the way the bedroom in the palace was decorated. The way that it was laid out. It was clear to her now that the palace really wasn't him.

He had said as much. Had said that he preferred to live in these other places. But she hadn't realized just how little of him was reflected in that bedchamber.

The far wall of the penthouse was made up entirely of windows, a glittering view of the city lights spread out before them. The furniture was low profile, black and brushed steel. The floors were very shiny black tile, so clean she could see her reflection in them. In fact, if Andres was paying attention, he would probably be able to use them to look up her skirt. She had to wonder then if that was actually their purpose.

She was not the first woman he had brought here, that was for certain.

Perhaps the floor tiles were all a part of the den of iniquity this place clearly was.

"You do not look entirely impressed," he said, closing the door behind him and walking deeper into the room.

"It is different. That's all."

"It's more than that. Your lip is nearly curling." He arched an eyebrow. "You disapprove."

"I was just pondering the finish on the tiles."

"What about it?" He set the bag that contained the cake on the end table by the couch.

"I wondered if you keep it so shiny so you can...see beneath dresses and things."

Much to her surprise he laughed. "No, that isn't why. Though I very much like the way your mind works. It seems a little bit twisted. Which I can appreciate."

"It was nothing more than logic. You have made me aggressively aware of your reputation."

"An interesting way of saying I have been honest with you."

A shiver racked her frame and she wrapped her arms around herself. "If you say so."

"I would never want to deceive you." He closed the distance between them, tracing her cheekbone with the edge of his thumb. "You have been so protected."

"You always say that. But you forget. I know I spent a long time separated from society. In borderline isolation. But it doesn't erase the tragedy that I experienced. It doesn't take away that pain. Once you understand the evil people are willing to commit, you're never the same. I have no experience of men and relationships, but I have seen the worst of people. The very worst. Yet I'm still breathing. I'm still standing. I am not someone in need of protection. Though your valor is appreciated."

"I do think you're the first person to ever accuse me of possessing valor."

"At least I can be a first for you in some way." She closed the distance between them, pressing a kiss to his lips.

"You seem jealous."

She frowned. "Maybe I am."

"A bit possessive."

"Probably that too. But I don't think it's incredibly unreasonable that I should dislike the idea of you being with other women."

"Of course not. But what made you think of it?"

"Being in this place. It is so clearly designed for seduction."

"It is. I won't lie to you." Her stomach fell further still. "It is, however, new and I have not yet had the chance to seduce anyone in it."

She felt more boosted from that than she should. "Oh."

"Does that please you?"

She curled her fingers around his tie, holding him close to her. "Yes, it really does."

"You surprise me."

"I surprise myself. But I have never wanted anything bad enough to try and lay exclusive claim to it. You are the exception."

"I don't usually like it when women get possessive of me. I feel, perhaps you are the exception for me, as well."

"I like the idea of that."

"You know what I like the idea of?" He released his hold on her and took one step back. "I like the idea of you taking that dress off."

"I thought you were supposed to be a master of seduction. Why should I be put in the position of seducing you?"

He loosened his tie and she was mesmerized by the movement. By the slide of the silk through the knot, by the movement of his hand. He slipped it through his collar and let it fall to the floor before flicking two buttons on his shirt open. "Forgive me, Zara, but I had imagined I had already seduced you."

She smiled, surprised at how easy she found it. Then she reached behind her back, grabbing hold of the zipper tab on her silk dress and sliding it down. "Is that meant to imply that you are not already seduced? You are the one who was so desperate for me we had to rush here. We had to come here instead of the palace because of your urgency."

She looked down, at the clear outline of his arousal pushing against the front of his trousers.

"Oh, yes," she said, "I think it's quite clear that I've already seduced you. You have seduced a great many women. You've told me yourself. I feel that I deserve to be part of that seduction."

"I washed your hair, woman. Was that not seductive?"

"I am, it turns out, a very jealous beast. No. Your hair washing was not sufficient. I demand more." She shrugged her shoulders and let her dress fall down into a silken pool at her feet. She was wearing nothing more than her very flimsy bra, panties and a pair of very bright red high heels that accentuated the shape of her legs. She did not feel embarrassed, or exposed. She felt powerful. Because she could see the heat in his eyes, see the tension in his body. She knew that he wanted her. She was certain of this, certain of him. At least in this moment. It was enough. For now, it was enough.

He slipped his black jacket off, casting it onto the couch that was near him. He unbuttoned the cuffs on his sleeves, pushing both up over his forearms. "I see. And what will it take to seduce you?"

"Take your shirt off. Slowly."

He said nothing, his hands going to the front of his shirt, slipping buttons through the holes just as she had instructed. With each movement he revealed more tan, toned skin, more rippling muscle. She bit her lip to keep a whimper from escaping. The truth was, she had been seduced ages ago, and there was no need to do it again. She just wanted it. Just because.

Another new decadence she was not accustomed to. Having something just because it felt good. Just because it made her happy.

When he was finished, he sent it the same way as his tie, his muscles bunching and shifting with the motion. Her mouth dried, her heart pounding hard against her breastbone, echoing in her head.

"Now your pants."

He arched a dark brow, his hands going to his belt, working it through the buckle slowly. She stared, transfixed. Everything about him was impossibly sexy. His chest, his stomach, arms, hands. She bit her lip thinking about what he was about to reveal. She was very excited about that too.

"You can go a little faster than this."

She was sure she wasn't imagining that, as soon

as she spoke the words, he slowed his movements. "Can I? Feeling impatient?"

Yes, yes, she was. "Not particularly."

"Are you sure I haven't already seduced you?"

"Keep trying, I say."

He smiled again. A genuine smile. She was keeping count of how many she had earned.

He rolled his shoulders back, the motion creating movement throughout the rest of his body. Movement she could not ignore. He was beautiful. No wonder women lost their heads over him. In truth, she imagined all he had to do was smile and he could have any woman thoroughly seduced with the beauty of his physical form. She would be more surprised if anyone ever resisted.

She certainly did not plan to resist.

He undid the closure on his pants, pushing them down his muscular thighs before straightening, revealing the full scope of his arousal. Hard and thick, and just for her.

"Sit down," she said, the words tumbling out of her mouth before she had a chance to process them.

He said nothing, but his expression asked a very clear question.

"Do not argue with me," she said, affecting her most imperious tone.

He took a couple of steps backward before sinking down onto the couch, his posture easy. He looked very much like a Roman emperor awaiting tribute. Well, as it so happened, she had a fitting tribute in mind.

She started to walk toward him slowly, conscious of the way her high heels made her hips sway as she walked, conscious of the way his eyes followed the motion. She stopped in front of him, taking a moment to simply admire his beauty. His square jaw, sensual mouth. Broad, muscular chest, and the dark hair that lightly covered his skin.

Then she slowly sank down to her knees, placing her palms on his thighs, her lips close to that most masculine part of him. She could only assume that as he had done this for her, and she had found it immeasurably pleasurable, the return would be just as successful.

She leaned in, examining him, her heart thundering. She ached for him already, her breasts feeling hypersensitive, needy for his touch. But she would have to wait. She would have to be patient. He had done what she'd asked. Exactly what she'd asked. And now she felt the need to demonstrate her appreciation.

She wasn't completely sure where to start, so she figured following instinct was the best way to go. She tilted her head, sliding the flat of her tongue along the hardened length of his shaft. She was startled by the forceful feeling of his fingers in her hair, holding her suddenly, tightly. "Zara," he said, his voice rough.

"Have I done something wrong?" she asked.

She was held immobile by his strong grip, unable to look at his face. Which was probably for the best. He had so much experience, it was very likely that her efforts were laughable, and she would have no idea. But he would. He would be well aware.

"No. But you don't have to…"

"I want to."

He groaned, and though he didn't release his hold, he loosened it. She leaned in again, returning to her original plan, taking a long, leisurely taste of him. She heard air hiss through his teeth, and she chose to take it as a positive sign, continuing in her exploration of his body. She shifted positions, wrapping her hand around the base of him, holding him steady as she took him into her mouth. He was soft, and smooth, but very hard. Hot. Not at all like what she'd imagined.

The desperation returned. The desire to know every bit of him. Every part of him.

She took him in deeper, relishing the breathy, uncontrolled sound of pleasure that he made. Paying close attention to the way his thigh muscles began to shake beneath her hand. She could feel his tension, running through every line of his body. Feel it echoing within her.

And suddenly, this wasn't enough. She needed more of him. All of him. She slowly rose to her feet, unhooking her bra and casting it to the floor before gripping the sides of her panties and drawing them down her legs, kicking them to the side. She decided to leave the shoes on, if only because it felt like a strange, illicit novelty.

She approached the couch, bending at the waist and gripping the back of it, just behind his shoulders, before lifting one knee and planting it beside his thigh, then doing the same with the other.

He growled, wrapping one arm around her waist, the other pressed against her shoulder blades, his hand buried in her hair. He pulled her down so that her mouth met his, his kiss fierce, uncontrolled.

Incredible.

He slid the hand that was resting on her back down to cup her bottom, then down farther between her thighs, stroking her slick flesh, teasing her entrance. She shivered, her legs growing weak, her stomach tight with need.

He pushed one finger inside her as he lowered his head and sucked a nipple deep into his mouth. The burst of pleasure exploded a pop of stars behind her eyes. It was so intense, so incredibly perfect. She wanted to ask him where he'd learned to do that, how he knew. But also, she didn't want to know.

And she wouldn't have been able to speak right now anyway.

He withdrew his finger, gripping her hips tight and positioning her over his arousal. "Now, Princess," he said, his teeth clenched tightly together.

She lowered herself slowly onto him, relishing the feel of him filling her inch by beautiful inch. And once she was seated fully onto him, she simply stopped, relishing the feel. Relishing the sensation of being connected to another person. As close as they could be.

She took a deep breath, and opened her eyes, meeting his. Oh, she wasn't just connected to anyone. She was connected to Andres. Her throat felt swollen, tight. And everything inside her felt right.

She couldn't remember the last time she'd felt as though she was at home. There had been the palace in Tirimia, but she couldn't even think of it without feeling fear. Grief. Sadness. And the camp, with the clan, it had never been home. They had never been family. Protectors. Valued. But it wasn't the same. It wasn't this.

And it wasn't Petras, or the palace here, and it certainly wasn't this penthouse with the Peeping Tom floors.

It was him. Andres. Home was the place you always wanted to return to. He was where she wanted to return to. Always. No matter where he was, whether it was in a castle or a hovel, then it would be home.

"I... Oh, Andres."

She couldn't say anything more. Couldn't get out the words that were swirling around inside her head. It was for the best. She was sure of that. She doubted it even made sense at the moment. She couldn't even make sense of the things rioting around inside her.

He held her tightly, guiding her movements with his hands. She followed for a while, before establishing her own rhythm, rolling her hips forward as she raised herself up slightly, teasing them both by going slow. It was torture for her. She wanted nothing more than to close her eyes and ride him hard and fast until they both found release. But she didn't want it to end.

She so didn't want it to end.

She rocked back and forth, gratified when a tortured sounding moan escaped his lips, when his hands tightened on her hips, his fingertips digging into her flesh, hard enough that she imagined it might leave a mark. She hoped it did. She hoped that she wore evidence of this claiming when it was finished. That the stubble from his five-o'clock shadow left her skin red, that she would be able to see the impressions of his hands where he had held her tight.

She rocked against him again, and this time he

growled. Feral, uncontrolled. As though she had brought him down to her level. She was always doing that. In the hall, in public at the palace, here in this place. But she wasn't sorry.

She liked him like this. Uncontrolled, needing her. Wanting her as she wanted him.

No walls between them. Nothing separating them.

She felt at home. Finally.

He held more tightly on to her, and suddenly, she was being propelled backward. He lowered her slowly to the floor, settling between her thighs and thrusting into her hard and deep. She felt tied to the spot, trapped beneath his strength and weight. And she loved it.

His dark eyes bored into hers, and she was certain he could see all her secrets. See down deep. She wanted him to. She wanted him to untangle all the frightening, intense emotions that were brewing inside her, because she wasn't certain if she could. She had no experience with this. Perhaps he did. He'd had lovers. Perhaps this was normal.

No.

Her heart rejected that thought. Immediately. Violently.

This wasn't like his other times. She was certain of that. Because he had said he felt nothing with Francesca. Because he was with so many different women, so often. There was no way it could be this feeling. This, all the time and with different people, would surely consume a person. Which would surely eat him alive from the inside out.

It was only him, and only her, and still it was going to devour her.

He held tightly to her hips as he drove deep. The tile was cold, hard beneath the bare skin of her back, but she didn't care. She was with Andres, and so she felt perfect. Even though her skin felt too tight for her body, even though all the things in her chest felt too large to be contained. Somehow there was all of that, and still she was perfect.

Everything with him was like that. Contradicting each other, complementing each other, being too much, not enough and yet just right.

The pleasure that was blooming in her stomach grew, expanded. She couldn't breathe, could scarcely handle the sensation that was spreading through her veins, bleeding outward, crackling over her skin like an electric current.

Andres lowered his head, his hold on her tightening as he growled, pushing inside her one last time as he found his release. That added pressure, the intensity of his own pleasure, heightened her own and she found herself letting go. Color flashing, exploding behind her eyelids as pleasure wrapped itself around her, cushioning her from everything. The past, the future, the hardness of the floor. There was nothing but Andres. Nothing but the two of them together. Nothing but the blinding, white-hot pleasure she experienced at his hands.

She screamed, losing control, utterly and completely as the intensity of her climax shook her. She screamed as she hadn't done since those lonely days when she was in the mountains by herself. Consumed by grief. Withering in her isolation. But this was different.

Before, she had only been able to make noise like that because she was alone. Because there was no one there to see.

But he was here. And she was free.

And when she came back to herself, she wasn't alone.

CHAPTER TEN

"WHERE HAVE YOU been the past couple of days? You disappeared during my speech. Don't think I didn't notice."

Andres stopped in the middle of the hall, closing his eyes and gritting his teeth at the sound of his older brother's voice coming from behind him. "I've been in Vegas. Gambling with the crown jewels. I traded our mother's engagement ring for a prostitute. Don't worry, she was very skilled."

"You can't have done that, because my wife wears that ring. Otherwise it sounds like you."

"I've been in my city apartment. With Zara. Did you think she was off in her room shredding newspaper and making a little mouse nest all this time?" He was being unnecessarily cruel to his brother, who probably had genuine concerns that Andres truly had been off whoring around. But for some reason, Andres was incapable of simply backing down in calming Kairos's fears.

"I have scarcely seen her since I put her in your custody."

"Convenient for you. You pass the woman off to me, and wash your hands of her completely. And trust me with attempting to tame her."

"And how has that been going?"

Andres allowed himself to think back on the past few days with Zara. They had barely left his apartment. They had barely dressed; they had eaten the entire cake he'd brought from the restaurant. Licked much of the frosting from her skin and shown her just what *having your cake and eating it too* could mean.

He had put on the bare minimum to receive food when it was delivered to the penthouse, but that was it. Otherwise he had preferred that they stayed naked. So that he had easy access to Zara at all times. In bed, on the kitchen counter, in the shower...

He had never felt so insatiable for a woman. This was unlike anything he'd ever known. It wasn't about filling a void with sex; it was about being with her. It wasn't a hunger for companionship in a general sense, but for Zara.

That realization left him feeling raw. She seemed happy with him.

Part of him wanted to hold on to that. To keep her with him. To use her as a cover for that empty well in his soul.

Zara didn't know the man he had built himself up to be. Didn't know the playboy who had done his best to destroy his brother's trust in him. The restless, uncontrollable boy who had driven off his mother. The man who only ever spent the night with his lovers to avoid being alone because he feared isolation more than any monster lurking in the shadows.

"It's been going well." He held up his hands, palms facing Kairos. "I'm still in possession of all ten fingers, so there's that."

"She's supposed to be your fiancée. Could you not talk about her like she's some sort of rabid mongrel?"

"I could," he said, thinking back to all the ways she was nothing of the kind, but a whole, pure woman. "But this is more fun."

"Are you going to be able to handle yourself when we announced your holiday wedding at the Christmas Eve party tonight?"

"I promise you, Zara and I have figured out how to deal with each other." He couldn't suppress the smile that turned up his lips.

Kairos raised his eyebrows. "Have you?"

"We have." And the deeper they settled into it, the more she wound herself around his life, the more unsettled he became.

Strange. He should take comfort in not being alone. But there was something about all this that made him feel as if he were being held underwater. As if he were holding her down with him.

And the deeper they went, the more panicked he felt. The more he wanted to release his hold on her and make his escape.

To retreat to the punishment of solitude because it would be better than the alternative.

Needing her. Losing her.

Failing her.

"Please tell me you didn't take her to Vegas to purchase hookers, as well."

"Oh, nothing as salacious as that. We're sleeping with each other. *Only* each other. Shocking. I suppose I should be grateful that you're married, and faithful to Tabitha. Otherwise this would be a wonderful chance for you to exact revenge."

In that moment he knew he would kill his brother if he so much as looked at Zara. Any man, really. What was wrong with him? He felt torn in two. Desperate to hold her to him. Desperate to let her go.

Unable to do either.

"It would be. But I wouldn't do that. Not to you. I'm not angry at you, whatever you might think. Well, I am. But not bitter. I'm not happy about what happened five years ago. How could I be? If I was deliriously satisfied in my marriage, perhaps it would be a different story."

"All the Christmas trees in the ballroom are decorated."

Both Andres and Kairos turned at the sound of Tabitha's stilted voice coming from the opposite direction. It was impossible to tell whether or not she had heard what Kairos had just said, but judging by the way her pale blue eyes glistened, and the lack of color in her cheeks, she most certainly had.

Andres had to wonder why Kairos found being married to a woman as beautiful as Tabitha such a hardship. She was completely biddable, nothing like Zara, who was obstinate and imperious on the best days.

Of course, that was what he found so fascinating about her. Perhaps that explained it. Perhaps Kairos had wanted a woman more like Francesca. Beautiful, impetuous. Very likely to leave her husband, or get pregnant with the royal stable master's baby rather than her husband's, but certainly possessing charms. Poor Tabitha would never be able to compete if that was what Kairos really wanted.

Tabitha was like a china doll who stored herself on the top shelf, ensuring that she remained thoroughly unplayed with, undamaged.

Though Andres suspected this had damaged her a bit.

"Thank you," Kairos said, his tone stiff. "I will be in to see everything in a moment. Andres and I were just talking."

"Then I'll leave you to it." She pushed her lips upward into a poor approximation of a smile before nodding once and turning away, walking back into the ballroom.

"You were saying?" Andres asked.

"Nothing. Only that I'm not actively rooting against you. I never have. You can make this work with her. Especially if you have a physical connection. So do it. Don't mess it up."

"I'm not a child, Kairos."

"Nor were you a child when you took my fiancée to bed."

"That is true."

"For once in your life, listen to someone."

He listened. He listened well. It had just never made a difference.

"She's a good woman," Kairos said. "Strong. She'll make a wonderful princess. And a wonderful wife."

She would. Andres couldn't argue with that. More than that…he wanted it. This time with her had been beyond anything he'd ever experienced. He hadn't wanted to connect with anyone like this in longer than he could remember.

But Zara…he took joy in caring for her. Giving to her. That was new too. Wanting to give to someone rather than simply take all he could.

The desperation he felt, so sudden, so intense, to cling to her nearly brought him to his knees.

It reminded him of every other time he'd wanted something, only to make a mess of it.

As he would do with Zara.

He pushed the thought away. He had no choice

but to succeed with her. But that didn't mean surrendering to this…thing, this emotion that rioted through his chest.

They could work together. They could be partners. It didn't have to be like this.

He would explain it to her. Tonight, after the ball, he would explain to her how it would be. A partnership. No feelings. Nothing so unstable, nothing so powerful.

A commitment, a decision, he could control. But he had proved to himself over and over that his heart was unreliable.

He took a breath and looked at Kairos. "If you'll excuse me," he said, turning away from his brother, "my fiancée is waiting for me. And she isn't mad at me."

"Give it time. And, Andres…"

"What?"

"If you leave during my speech tonight I will be unhappy with you."

"Then make it interesting."

Tonight, she was wearing the pink gown. That fluffy confection that had been fitted to her the first day she was here in the palace. Her dark hair had been tamed into a sleek bun, a tiara resting on her head.

It was so foreign. Yet familiar at the same time. This had been her life once. Parties, beautiful dresses, crowns. She had been royalty in the palace and Tirimia. In her daily life she had only ever felt the distance of royalty, and none of the benefits.

This was different. Tonight, she would stand with the entire royal family. Part of something. Not apart from something. Tonight, Kairos would be announcing that she and Andres were getting married after the Christmas service tomorrow morning, in the old church down in the city.

The most beautiful dress had been created for her. Zara could scarcely believe it had been made up so quickly. It glittered like the snow that fell here in Petras. Lace with little glass beads stitched all over it.

She couldn't think of anything more beautiful to wear while becoming Andres's wife. And she couldn't think of anything more beautiful to wear tonight for when the country found out she was becoming his wife.

And all of it mattered more because she had realized something over the course of the past few days spent in his penthouse. She loved him.

She had no experience of love, that much was true. She didn't even remember what it felt like to be loved by a family. But that was why she knew what this was. She imagined you never appreciated food more than you did when getting it after you'd been starving. That everything tasted better, each bite more precious, worthy of savoring. You didn't need to have experience of feasts to understand that you were dining at an exquisite table.

She knew. Knew that this was everything she'd been waiting for.

She'd thought of it as home the other day. Thought of him as home. Had thought of this as destiny, the fulfillment of the promise of her royal birth. She could see now it was more than that. The feeling people talked about when they discussed their homes was love. And as much as you could love a place, she loved a person so much more.

Andres.

Her first foray out of the woods. Her first real human connection, in so long.

Being with him was more healing than time or distance. Being with him, choosing him, forced her to realize that while the clan had certainly been distant, she had been distant, as well.

It wasn't until Andres that she had reached out.

"Are you ready?"

She turned and saw Andres standing there, looking perfect in an expertly tailored tux. A striking black jacket, a matching bow tie and a crisp white shirt. He was clean shaven, his dark hair brushed off his forehead. He looked less rakish than usual, but he was as devastatingly sexy as ever.

He was going to be her husband. He really was hers, to keep. The very idea made her giddy down to her bones.

She couldn't recall ever being giddy in her life before this.

"Yes. Ready."

"This is a massive party. And the service tomorrow will be even bigger. I hope you feel adequately prepared."

"I don't know if it's possible to feel prepared for an event on this magnitude. But I'm not going to revert to an animalistic state and hide under a table."

"Well, that is reassuring. Though I must say I wasn't particularly concerned." He held his hand out and she took it, electricity sparking over her fingertips, straight to her heart as their skin made contact and he pulled her close. He kissed her and the world fell away. "We will have to dance, though."

"I'm ready if you are."

He smiled. "I'm always ready."

She slipped her hand down between them, cupping his arousal. "I know you are."

A rough sound vibrated in his chest. "You can't do that. We have to go. Kairos will notice if we're late."

"I suppose it's bad form to upset the king. Especially if he's about to be your brother-in-law."

"Very good advice." He kissed her cheek, then looped his arm through hers, turning them both toward the door. "Advice I would like to ignore."

"Poor Andres. Forced to behave."

"We'll see how long it lasts," he said. His tone was dry, but it wasn't as full of humor as his voice often was. There was something strange beneath it. Something she couldn't identify.

"Do I have to worry about you gnawing on chicken bones?"

He grinned, his expression wicked, and she was forced to admit she might have been imagining the strangeness in his earlier statement. "Possibly. You never can tell."

They walked down the hall together, staff members bustling to get out of their way as they made their way through the corridors, down to the ballroom. The entire entry to the castle had been transformed. Great boughs of holly and evergreen were draped over banisters, hung over doorways. White lights twinkled on every surface, peeking out from the dark green trees and decorations, giving everything a special glow.

Zara couldn't remember the last time she had celebrated Christmas like this. Couldn't remember the last time she'd seen a Christmas tree until this week. They did not celebrate in the same fashion in the clan. It wasn't part of the traditions. They had celebrated at the palace, and all of this was like a vague, foggy fantasy come to brilliant, glittering life before her eyes.

"It's magical."

She looked back at Andres, who looked as though he was suppressing laughter. "I'm very glad you like it."

"It's my first Christmas party in…ever. My parents used to throw them at the palace in Tirimia. But I wasn't invited because I was too young."

"Well, you aren't too young now."

"No."

"Let's go inside. Wait until you see the ballroom."

He led her inside, and she couldn't help responding to his enthusiasm. As if she needed any encouragement. The ballroom was stunning, trees stationed every few feet, in a circle around the dance floor, tables situated between. White lights were strung between them, casting a net of stars over the partygoers. It was as if a little snow globe had been captured, enclosed by the ballroom rather than glass and water.

"It's beautiful. Really beautiful." She turned and smiled at him. "I think that sounds silly. Like not enough. I'm being obvious, I know. But I don't know what else to say."

"That's how I feel when I try to compliment you." His dark eyes were serious, and it made her stomach tighten. Made her heart beat faster.

Made her wonder if maybe, just maybe, he loved her too.

Andres moved easily through the crowd, greeting everyone they encountered. They were congratulated by countless people, because while they had not made a formal announcement of the engagement, it was being treated as common knowledge. People of course didn't know the circumstances surrounding their engagement, but Zara imagined it didn't really matter now. Not now that their relationship was real.

"Shall we take our seats?" he asked.

Zara nodded, and let him lead her to a table at the far end of the ballroom that allowed those sitting at it to get a view of the entire proceedings. Kairos, Tabitha and a few people Zara had never seen before were already seated there.

Andres leaned in. "Diplomats. Politicians. It will be a very dry table."

"I think we'll manage."

"This will be your life. These kinds of parties. This sort of company."

She tried to make sense of his words. Tried to figure out if any of it mattered. If she cared one way or the other. "Well, it will have you too. So the rest doesn't really matter."

He drew back, frowning. "I wouldn't count on me being one of the perks, Princess."

"I've spent quite a bit of time with you over

the past week. There are a great many perks to you."

"Perhaps to my body. To what I can do to yours. As a human being I tend to fall short."

She frowned, matching his. "I've yet to see evidence of that."

He said nothing, rather he continued over to the table, so she followed him. She was irritated with him. It had been a while since he was irritating. Or perhaps, she had simply been insulated by the good things he made her feel. That was entirely possible. He did make her feel some very good things.

She took a seat beside Andres, with Tabitha on her other side. The queen was very quiet, and very purposefully not looking at her husband. Zara had to wonder again if this was her fate, inescapably. It was this relationship, so clearly strained, that had made her nervous at the last meal they'd shared. She had been so convinced recently that she and Andres had something entirely different, but then, there were these moments when he would shut down on her completely, and she wasn't entirely sure after that.

As with everything else at the party, the meal was lovely. Zara mainly listened to people talk about topics she wasn't very informed on. Andres seemed to be doing the same. Zara turned to Tabitha. "Did you enjoy dinner?" Probably a silly question to ask the queen, who very likely had planned the menu. But she was hopeless at talking to women. She had not had very many friends in her life, Andres was the closest thing, and he wasn't a woman. Far from it.

Zara found that she very much wanted to make Tabitha a friend. Another thing that was within her reach, thanks to this arrangement.

"Yes," Tabitha said, seemingly unruffled by Zara's clumsy attempt at conversation.

"Everything is lovely." She knew she sounded stilted, but she was trying. "It's been a very long time since I've celebrated Christmas. Since I've seen Christmas decorations, and never anything like this. I love Christmas." She hadn't let herself remember how much, because it was only painful. Something else to add to the sad, empty ache. Another thing she missed that she couldn't have back.

"Do you?" Tabitha tilted her head to the side, the words brittle.

"Yes. Doesn't everyone?"

"I find it quite stressful, I confess."

Zara noticed Tabitha sneak a quick glance at Kairos.

"A lot of planning. A lot of smiling."

Tabitha wasn't doing a very good job of smiling at the moment.

"I can see how it might be. I'm used to... Well, people don't usually pay so much attention to me."

"You don't find it daunting?"

"Not when I'm with him," Zara said, a blush rising in her cheeks.

Tabitha arched her eyebrows. "Andres?"

"Yes. He's at ease in every situation. I can't help being at ease too."

"So things are…going well between the two of you?"

If Zara wasn't mistaken, there was a slight edge to Tabitha's voice now.

"Yes." Zara shifted uncomfortably. "He's been very good to me. He cares for me—"

"I see," Tabitha said, clipped.

Andres chose that moment to lean over and whisper in her ear, "Zara, it looks like the dance floor is beginning to fill. Would you like to join me for a dance?"

"Yes," she said, grateful for the chance to escape. She had done something wrong. She supposed she shouldn't be too surprised. She had no experience with any of this. She was moving through it all blindly, having faith that it would work out because she was enjoying herself. Because she was happy. But of course Tabitha had friends. She was secure in her place. Just because Zara desperately wanted the connection didn't mean that Tabitha did.

Oh, all of this was so complicated.

She accepted Andres's hand and led the charge

to the dance floor, eager to escape her embarrassment.

Once they were out in the center, she buried her head in his chest as he wrapped his arm around her waist and took hold of her hand, holding her close to his body. "What's wrong?" he asked.

"Oh, I think I made a mess of things with Tabitha."

"Tabitha is difficult to connect with sometimes. She's quite controlled."

"She wasn't so much in this instance. I think it upset her that our relationship is going so well."

He frowned, and her stomach twisted. She felt as though she'd said something wrong again. What if he didn't think their relationship was going well?

There were so many uncertainties in all this. Insecurity had never been something she'd had to contend with before. She had been lonely back with the clan, but she had known exactly where she stood. Everyone had positive feelings about her; it was just that a protocol dictated they keep their distance. There was no wondering. People said what they meant; they didn't play guessing games. With their mouths saying one thing and their eyes clearly communicating another.

"I think she is in a difficult position with Kairos at the moment."

Zara was relieved to hear that, and she realized

that a knot of tension had formed in her stomach that she had scarcely been aware of until it began to loosen. She hadn't imagined that Andres had anything going on with Tabitha, not really, but she had been worried about it somewhere in the back of her mind until he'd said that. Love was making her slightly crazy. Especially with all the things that were unsaid. That was just how people seemed to do things here. That was how this family seems to do things.

She didn't understand it.

She would have to, though. She would have to figure all this out somehow. Because she might need only Andres, but he came with a host of issues she would have to negotiate. Loving him meant navigating all this, and so she would. She had not survived a siege on her palace, loss and loneliness, to come out the other side weak and frightened. She had strengths. And she would use them here.

When necessary. Right at this moment, she didn't need them. Being in his arms didn't require strength. When she was in his arms, she was able to lean on him. A beautiful thing, since she had never been able to do that growing up. There had been no one for her to lean on. There had been only herself. The two of them would be much stronger. When the winds blew they could stand strong together.

That truth, that belief, was suddenly so strong inside her, burning with so much conviction that she could not hold it in any longer.

"Andres... I need to tell you something."

"You didn't stash your dinner in a potted plant, did you?" he asked, his voice full of humor.

"No," she said, pressing her forehead to his shoulder. "Nothing like that. I just need to tell you... I'm looking forward to becoming your wife tomorrow."

She felt him stiffen in her arms. "Well, this is a good thing," he said, "as no matter your feelings on the subject, you *will* become my wife tomorrow."

"I know. But I think that you should know that I want to be your wife. I'm happy here with you. I want to be a part of this, part of this family. I want to have your children. I want to be with you."

He stiffened further, pulling away from her slightly. "What brought this on?" His voice was guarded, his expression shuddered.

"Our time together," she said, feeling confused. "Things have changed between us. Surely you must see that."

"We are sleeping together, if that's what you mean."

"It's more than that."

"Is it? It might be for you, *agape*, but I can guarantee you that it isn't for me. I'm a man who has had many lovers, and this is all very run-of-the-mill as far as I'm concerned."

There was something off about his tone. It didn't sound like him. It didn't feel like him. These words didn't feel real. She knew Andres. Knew the glitter he got in his eye when he was enjoying himself, knew when his smiles were genuine and when they were forced. This was forced. As forced as any one of his fake shows of happiness and ease. He was trying to upset her, and she couldn't fathom why.

"It's different. What's between us," she insisted, "I know it is. It isn't just sex."

His lips curved upward, his expression unkind. "The virgin thinks she knows whether or not this is just sex?"

"As you said, I'm not even *almost* a virgin anymore."

He chuckled, the sound flat, bitter. Sharp enough to cut straight through her skin. To pierce her chest. "Yes, I may have said that, but emotionally, you are much closer to a virgin than you are to a siren."

"Why are you being like this?"

"I'm not being like anything. This is who I am. This is *what* I am. I was honest with you from the beginning. You know what manner of man I am. The kind of man who would sleep with his brother's fiancée close enough to his brother's wedding that it created a need for that brother to marry a woman he barely knew, much less loved."

"Oh."

"All that Kairos and Tabitha are going through now? All that strain you see? That pain? That's on me. They never should have been together. It was never supposed to be the two of them. But I ruined things between Kairos and Francesca. So here we are. Here you are. Because of me."

"But I... I'm happy to be here. I love you, Andres."

Given the direction of the conversation, she didn't know what possessed her to make that admission. And yet she hadn't been able to keep it inside, not for another moment. She did love him, and she needed him to know it.

Did Andres believe that anyone loved him? She didn't think he did. More than that, he didn't love himself. She realized then, with blinding certainty, that he hated himself. That was why he was always telling her how bad he was, why he was always trying to reinforce the fact that he was no good.

He couldn't love himself, so she would do it for him.

This went beyond destiny. Beyond being a princess. Beyond simply being intended for palace life and a marriage to a prince. This was about being a woman. A woman who loved a man more than anything else.

This wasn't about running from loneliness or using him to fill a void. This was more than that.

He was more than that.

Had her life been full of love, had she been raised in the palace with her mother and father, she still would have needed him.

He would still have been a missing piece. It wasn't the palace, the position that was her destiny. It was him.

"I love you," she repeated.

The second use of the phrase seemed to jar him out of whatever trance he was in. "No."

"What?"

"There you go again, questioning everything I say. You heard me the first time. No, you cannot love me."

"Yes, I can. Because I do. That is not your decision to make."

"It's impossible. Maybe you have Stockholm syndrome. Or Overly Attached Fruit Basket syndrome, I don't know. But there's no way you can possibly love me. You were forced into being here with me. Forced into this arrangement."

"I certainly wasn't forced into your bed."

"Again, Princess, that is sex. It has nothing to do with love. Nothing to do with emotional connections."

"It does for me."

"Why?" he asked, his voice broken, fierce. "Why would you love me?"

She sensed that this was important. This was essential. That her answer carried with it the power to heal or the power to destroy.

She closed her eyes, shutting out the people around them, shutting out the Christmas trees, the glitter, the Christmas carols that were being played by the string quartet. She shut out all the beauty. All the trappings that came with Andres, so all that was left was him. Them.

And she wasn't alone. Not anymore. She wasn't afraid.

"You remember how my childhood was. I lost my parents. My brother. I was so isolated. And I feared sometimes that I would die from it. That the hole inside my chest would one day expand so great that it would swallow me up. That there would be nothing left of me. People were all around me, but none of them touched me. None of them loved me. I have been starving for years. I have been starving for you. It has nothing to do with sex, though I enjoy what we have together. It's more. It has everything to do with the fact that we are the same. My soul recognizes yours, Andres. And when I met you, I met the other part of myself."

He made a derisive, dismissive sound. "We are

not the same. Little one, you are an innocent from an enchanted wood. I am the most hardened man whore you could ever hope to run across. I am the man who mothers warn their daughters about. I am the one who makes husbands fear for their wedding vows. I am jaded and cynical. I have indulged in every manner of vice imaginable. Tell me, how is it you think we're the same?"

"Because we were alone."

He stopped moving then. The music played on, but she and Andres were frozen in the middle of the floor.

"I have never been alone in my life. I was born in a palace staffed by hundreds of people. I had nannies, more than one, from the beginning. I was never without friends at school. I never go to bed alone unless I choose to. I go to more parties in a year than most people will attend in their entire lives. Even when I was left in my room while my parents went to dinner parties, I was surrounded by people waiting to cater to my every whim."

"That is survival, Andres. Not love. Not truly being with people. You were the one who told me that."

"No, you mistake me, Princess. I have never once been alone, not like you."

"Why do you punish yourself with isolation? Why did you run from me when we made love against the wall? Because you know, as I do, that being alone is the most powerfully frightening thing. You know, because you have been." Her voice was muted, but her conviction remained. She was certain what she was saying was right. That it was true. "You're lonely. As lonely as I have been. But instead of going into the woods to scream about your isolation, you buried yourself in the nearest available vice. You tried to make yourself believe you weren't alone because there were people around to help you do it. I didn't have that option, so I had to accept my loneliness. Learn to understand it. You've been lying to yourself. You're hurting. And nobody really knows you. Nobody else realizes."

"Countless women *know* me, in the biblical sense, which I imagine is a much stronger sense than a great many other versions of *knowing* someone."

"Stop it. You put on this air of cynicism, you act like no one can touch you. Like nothing matters. But it's a lie. I know it is. Because I've seen you. I have never gone and read about your past. Everything I know about what a terrible person you are has come from you. It's come from your own lips. But I don't believe it. I never have. I've never gone looking for anyone else's opinion on who you might be. I have formed my own. You are a good man. You love your brother. You love this country. If you didn't you wouldn't be trying to atone for your mistakes now. You are loyal. Stubborn. A little bit mean when you're angry, but only because you're protecting yourself. You have been generous with me. As a lover, as a friend. You have stayed with me, shown me things, treated me with exceeding care. You washed my hair. Andres, you are a good man. So many people have written stories about you, but who are they? Why do they matter? Let my opinion be enough. Believe that. If nothing else, believe me."

"You have known me for a matter of mere weeks, *agape*. Sadly your opinion of me, formed while I was on my best behavior, carries very little weight."

"So this was your best behavior, then? Not your regular behavior?"

"Yes," he said, his teeth grinding together.

"Fine. Then make it your behavior. If you can do it, then continue to do it."

"It will come to an end. It always does."

"It doesn't have to. We are getting married tomorrow. We're starting the first day of the rest of our lives. It's new for both of us. Make it new. Start again. With me."

"I need a drink." He released his hold on her, pushing himself backward and stalking off the dance floor, leaving her standing there alone, her heart pounding sickly in her chest.

She had ruined it. She couldn't figure out why,

or how. She only knew that she had. She would have died to hear him say that he loved her. She had assumed he must feel the same.

Perhaps being alone was better in many ways. If she were still alone she wouldn't have to deal with this pain. Deal with this hurt. As it was, she felt as if she was crumbling apart from the inside out.

She saw the dessert was being served at the table she and Andres had abandoned, and made the decision to go and sit back down.

She would give him a while, and then, once he had cooled off, she would go after him.

Andres couldn't breathe. He couldn't think. She couldn't love him. It was impossible. Oh, for one, heady second, he had let himself imagine that it might be true. And let himself imagine it would be something that he could take full advantage of. A wife who would adore him. Who thought he was good. What an incredible thing that would be. Sadly it was something he would only lose in the end. Because that was what happened. It was who he was. It was what he did. He drove people away. His mother. He'd made the best attempt he could with Kairos. And starting tomorrow, and on into eternity, he would be waiting. Waiting for that dangling sword to fall, to tear asunder all that he and Zara had built.

Perhaps it wouldn't be this year, or the next year. Perhaps it would not be until they'd had children. Children who would also look up to him, idolize him. Love him. Depend on him as he had done with his parents.

Children he wouldn't deserve. A wife he could never hope to deserve.

He would ruin things. For all of them. And in the years while he waited for the killing blow, he would drive himself crazy. Knowing it would come eventually, but never knowing when.

He was feeble. His spirit so corrupt he knew that he could never be the kind of man that she needed.

He wasn't Kairos. Who would lay down everything, personal happiness, individual goals, everything, to serve his country. To serve a wife he didn't even love. Andres could never be that noble. He had never managed to keep the love of another person. Not even his parents. His behavior always ruined it in the end. He had no control. He never had.

The past few weeks had been a game. And he had been indulging himself. But it had to end.

He had to show her now. Because it would be better to destroy everything before the wedding. Better now than years from now. So she knew where things would end. So she knew what to expect.

They had to marry; there was no question of that. But...he could not have her loving him.

He stopped at the edge of the ballroom, scanning the crowd. And then he saw her. A blonde woman in a red dress, her curves barely contained by the tight, silken material. She was exactly the kind of woman he would have put the moves on in the past. Exactly the kind of woman he would choose to spend a few hedonistic hours with once boredom set in at a party like this.

And for the first time in years he let himself remember that last Christmas party. His mother had given him another chance. Had allowed him to come down from his room.

This time as they'd sat at the table, a family, pretending to have unity for all the world to see, his actions had not been beyond his control.

He had been angry. Angry for the years he'd spent locked away. Angry at how long and hard he'd tried only to fail time and time again. To get lost in the endless cycle of trying to please someone who professed to love him and failing at every turn.

So he'd chosen to fail that day. Had thrown his dinner plate on the floor and smashed it to pieces. Had made his mother cry again. It had felt good to accomplish what he'd set out to do. To fail spectacularly on purpose, rather than to try and fall short.

And then she'd left after that. God help him, he'd been relieved. Because after that he'd never had to try again.

He looked up, saw his fiancée sitting at the table, her posture stiff, taking tiny bites of her dessert, trying to enjoy it, trying to listen to the conversation around her. She did not fit in, his Zara. She did not have that cultured manner of those raised in nobility. Did not have the social graces she would have learned had she been raised in the palace life.

She was utterly unique. Utterly *her*.

He drank in the sight of her. Pale skin, dark hair, in that pink and gold dress that made her look like something out of a fairy tale.

But he wasn't the sort of man who deserved a fairy tale.

He took a step forward. Then another. Then, he began to make his way toward the blonde. Toward temptation.

He was not going to wait for hell to come up and grab him. He would walk and willingly. And he would do it now.

CHAPTER ELEVEN

ZARA HADN'T SEEN Andres for at least fifteen minutes. He had slipped out of the ballroom at some point when she wasn't looking, and she hadn't seen him anywhere since. She knew he wasn't in the room, because she felt the change.

Perhaps that sounded ridiculous, but she could feel his presence. Because it carried such weight. That connection they shared. Years of being alone had made it stronger, she was convinced. Or maybe it was so for everyone in love.

Though when you were the only one in love, perhaps it wasn't.

She had been sitting at the table in utter silence, trying not to look as distressed as she felt, and probably failing miserably. She took a deep breath, standing, deciding that she was going to go find him now. She wasn't one to wait. She wasn't one to play games. And just because he seemed to prefer to operate with a thin veil of deceit between his words and his feelings did not mean she had to do it. She was going to force him to confront this. To discuss it. Because he was telling her lies, she was certain.

He felt more for her, for what they shared, than he claimed. She knew he did.

She strode through the ballroom, quite amazed that the crowd of people parted for her as they seemed to do for Andres. She really was a part of this place now. She was one of them.

Her happiness was dented by the situation she was in. It was very difficult to feel happy when your heart was ground to dust. Another new discovery. Though a rather logical one.

She left the ballroom, exiting the main double doors out the back, and finding herself in the corridor where she and Andres had first made love. She didn't know what had led her here, but now that she was here, she knew it had been for a reason. This would be where he'd go. She was certain of it.

She rounded the corner from the ballroom, headed toward that alcove where they had first found their passion. And then she heard voices, rustling.

She stopped. Listening for a moment.

Her stomach twisted, sank deep down, terror gnawing at her insides, and still, she walked forward. Because she had to. Because he was there. She knew it.

She took one step, then another, headed toward the alcove. And when she rounded the corner, everything stopped.

It was Andres. And a woman. The woman was wearing a bright red dress, a crimson stain against

Andres's black suit. She was crushed hard against his body. His arms were wrapped tightly around her, his lips pressed hard to hers. He shifted, angling his head, and she saw his tongue slide against hers.

A cry escaped Zara's lips and she clasped her hand over her mouth. The blonde jumped as though she'd been scalded, but Andres moved slowly, fluidly, raising his head in a lazy, laconic fashion, one eyebrow lifted.

"Zara." He said her name so blandly. As though he wasn't surprised. As though he wasn't sorry. "I wasn't expecting you."

"Clearly," she said, her tone vibrating with rage.

"I was a bit bored of the party."

"Is that what you do when you're bored at parties? Come out here and *have* women up against walls?"

"Don't be dramatic. Obviously I wasn't *having* her. Yet."

The blonde made a coughing sound, her expression irritated. "I didn't sign on for drama," she said. "Just a little bit of fun with the prince."

"Sorry," Zara said, not feeling sorry at all. "This prince comes with drama. A rather large amount of it. In the form of me."

"I shall leave you to it." The woman moved away from Andres, walking closer to Zara. The light fell across her beautiful face, and Zara could see her red lipstick, smudged over to her cheek. That was how passionately he had been kissing her.

She had been wrong earlier. She thought her heart had been broken already. Damage done. But no, there were apparently some pieces left to shatter. To be ground beneath the stiletto of another woman.

It was his fault. Not hers.

That made it even worse.

She waited until the blonde was out of sight before trying to formulate a sentence. She would not give the other woman the satisfaction of hearing how upset she was.

"You lied to me." The words were low, shaky. She felt as if they had cost her the very last bit of air in her lungs. As if she would pass out from the force it had taken to speak them.

"That's what I do. I told you. I'm just a selfish playboy. And I'm sorry, but in situations like this I revert to type. I didn't do it to hurt you."

"Lies!" The word exploded from her with deadly force. She had suddenly found her strength. As he stood there, looking at her, his expression bland as though he had not just reached inside her chest and reordered all the new, beautiful things she had just discovered, she had found her strength. Her will to stand up to him. Her will to fight.

"You did it to hurt me."

"Why would I? It's just that I leave casualties in my wake. It's what I do."

"No! It's what you choose to do!"

"Is there a difference?"

She took a step toward him, feeling fierce. Unafraid. She had nothing to lose. If Andres had been everything, then there was nothing to protect anymore. Because it was all gone.

"It is every difference. You are not at the mercy of this. You have made yourself this. You can blame no one but yourself."

"I can't blame the mother who walked out on me and the father who gave up on me?" he asked, his tone even. Far too smooth.

She wanted him broken.

"No. They did not fashion you. You fashioned yourself. You talk of it as though it is part of your legend. An amusing anecdote for you to throw out when it suits you, to put distance between yourself and your accuser. As if I will back away from you if I understand that you're nothing more than a little boy wishing his mommy would come back and hug him. But I will not," she said, her voice shaking. "I do not feel sorry for you. Because while your mother left you years ago, and while that certainly hurt you, you have been inflicting wounds upon yourself every day thereafter. That is not her fault. You cannot blame her anymore."

"The hell I can't."

"You are in a hell of your own making! You cannot accept the fact that anyone might stay with you and so you're intent on pushing everyone who loves you away. Why? Because one woman didn't love you?"

"The only woman who should have loved me, simply because I was drawing breath, didn't. That is an entirely different thing. And not only her. My father."

"So that means you must not be worthy of love? That means that you have to set out to prove that those of us who are foolish enough to care for you are in fact fools? Why do you insist on putting a gun to your own head?"

"I know what I am, that's all. There is no point in trying to refashion myself in a manner that I am unsuited to."

"Who says you are unsuited? I have been with you these past weeks and you are suited to me. Until now. Until you dared touch another woman when you swore to me you would not." Her throat tightened, pain lancing her. "You said that I would be the only one."

"Yes. And I meant it then. I did. But things change. And that's the way it is with me. I do not keep my word. I never have."

"You are a liar."

"No!" he roared back at her. "It is more than

that. I have never kept my word. And in the end? I didn't even try."

"What?" The question came out small, weak.

"I told my mother that at the Christmas Eve dinner I would behave myself. That she could allow me out of my room this time. I had made mistakes, so many in years past that my mother had issued a decree I could no longer partake in public events. I could never sit still. I could never listen to instructions. I was a very bad boy. Always. I ruined everything that she did. Every appearance we had to make with the family. She mourned my existence, Zara. My very birth. They should have stopped with Kairos. She knew it. She told me. But that last time…that last time I didn't even try. I broke my plate on purpose, made a mess of the table setting because I was so angry with her. And when she left I was glad because I would never have to try for her again."

"Andres…"

"No. Do not look at me with those pitying eyes, Zara. What can you possibly know about it? For years I tried my damnedest. But it was never good enough. So when I stopped trying, I didn't just stop trying. I did my best to be bad. To move so far past the point of redemption I could never be retrieved from beyond it. That's the man I am now. I give in freely to my vices. I rejoiced at the loss of my mother because it meant there was no one left to try and control me and I could happily sink into the depths of debauchery. Marry me tomorrow if you want, Zara. But I will never love you. And you will never be able to be certain of my fidelity. How can you be when I will never be certain of it? When I will never do a damn thing to resist my own desires. I spent too many years trying and failing. I would not do it for my mother and I sure as hell won't do it for you."

"You bastard. You utter bastard. I am *trapped* here with you. You made me love you. You presented to me the stark truth that I have no other options beyond marrying you, and now, now that you have forced me to care, you tell me that I cannot have you."

"Don't be silly. You can have me. You just can't have exclusive rights on me."

"Then I don't want you at all."

"You can have your distance, Zara. I will ensure that you are taken care of. I will ensure that everything you need is handled. We will keep up appearances…"

"No."

"Yes. And make no mistake, you will still be my wife. But you do not have to live with me. You do not have to love me."

"No. I will not be your wife. I cannot."

Andres ground his teeth together, his expression fierce. "I promised Kairos."

"You break every promise. You said you enjoy being beyond redemption. So you should very much like this. You should've known that you could not cross me without retribution. I will not be made a fool of."

"So you would not leave when you were given to me as a gift, a thing, but you will leave now for your pride?"

"Yes." The word fell from her lips softly, confidently. "Because I'm a different woman now than I was when I first came to you. I was afraid then. Afraid that if I left the palace, if I left your care, I would simply die out in a snowbank somewhere. Afraid to let anyone close because the loss might kill me. But I know that isn't true now. I'm stronger than that. I will leave here, and I will make a life for myself. Because I can. I can change. I can learn. I have shown myself that. But one thing I will not do is stay for this. This humiliation. This pain."

She turned away, her hand shaking. She swallowed hard. "I loved leaning on your strength, Andres. But I am capable of standing on my own."

"We are getting married tomorrow," he said, as though she hadn't spoken. "My brother is announcing it tonight."

"You should have thought of that before you betrayed me. I am not forgiving, Andres." She hadn't known that about herself. But now she did.

She'd never had her heart broken before, not quite in this manner.

It turned out she was slightly vindictive. "I will not forgive you for this. Kairos and the fallout are your problem. The wedding, and what happens when I fail to appear, is your problem."

She strode away from him, down the empty corridor, her high heels clicking on the marble, echoing in the space.

She rounded the corner, saw the two double doors that led outside and flung them open, bracing herself against the biting chill of the wind. It was snowing outside, a thick blanket of it covering the ground. She walked forward, wrapping her arms around herself, rubbing her bare skin with her hands. She could see her breath, and she became aware of a chill on her cheek.

She was crying. Tears falling down, leaving icy tracks behind. She looked back at the palace, and ahead at the blank canvas of white. She lifted up her full pink skirt and began to run through the snow as quickly as she could, her feet sinking deep into the icy cold, but she didn't care. She slipped, falling down onto her knee, and forward, her gown billowing out around her. She stopped, letting the cold seep through. Down her skin, down to her bones.

She shivered. The physical discomfort she felt did not compare to the pain that was rioting through her chest. To the unending darkness that was threatening to destroy her.

She leaned forward, the snow freezing her exposed skin. And she didn't care.

She knew she needed to get up. She knew she needed to run, as she had told him she would. She couldn't just lie here and die in a snowbank; that was an old fear. But, for a moment it was tempting.

And when she felt that flicker of temptation, she stood. No, she would not fade away. She would not hide herself from pain. She would not allow for herself to be alone. Not to protect herself, not for any reason at all. She would have what she wanted. No, she couldn't have Andres. But whether she stayed or left, that would be the case. She would not subject herself to that. And she was strong enough now to claim that for herself. To understand that she deserved it.

She had suffered far too much loss in her life. The loss of her parents hurt still, but if there was one thing she knew it was that you could survive grief. She could survive pain.

She could survive being alone.

She stood, walking to the garage, where she knew she would find the driver whom Andres had been using the past few weeks.

She saw him standing in there, by the car, obviously waiting for anyone who might need a ride.

He pushed away from the car, lifted his head. "Princess?"

"I need you to take me into town. I need to see Julia Shuler. Can you help me find her?"

It was not the best thing to be drunk on your wedding day. Hell, it probably wasn't the best thing to be drunk on Christmas Day. Christmas *morning*, if he were being completely precise. But he had not been able to find Zara after their confrontation last night, and so he had gone into his brother's library and made liberal use of the Scotch.

He was waiting for the pain, the headache to hit. Right now the buzz was all that lingered.

She would come today, he was confident in that. He had made a mistake last night, he knew that. He had gone one too far in using that woman to hurt Zara.

He had put off touching her for as long as possible, and when he had heard footsteps in the hallway he had grabbed her and pulled her into his embrace, kissing her. Deeply. Passionately. So that no one who bore witness could miss it.

He wasn't sure what he had expected, but he had not expected the repulsion that had crawled over his skin. He didn't want this other woman. She was beautiful, and yet he didn't want her. Did not want to taste her lips, did not want her lipstick lingering on his flesh.

And when Zara had seen him…

He had never known such regret. Not even when he had been confronted with the pictures of himself and Francesca.

But it had been too late, and he had done what he always did. He had lashed out and hurt her. He had doubled down on the reasoning behind his actions. His brain justifying himself all while his mouth issued the vilest insults to the person he should be prostrating himself before, begging for forgiveness.

He had felt so desperate to disappoint her now instead of later. Had felt so compelled to make her hate him early so that he had nothing to try and live up to. So that he wasn't surprised when she left.

What he hadn't counted on was the hurt in her eyes. His mother had never faced him after that final day. She had simply left. His father had met him with rage only. Kairos had had kind of a quiet acceptance about him, but had stood firm in the stance that they were brothers and nothing would break their bond.

Zara had made it very clear that their bond was broken. She had faced him down with anger, as his father had done. But there was more to it than that. It was a righteous anger, and not for herself…for him. Because she had expected that he was better. Truly.

He realized right then that his parents never had expected more from him.

He had willingly disappointed them, because that was living down to their expectations. Zara was the only one who had truly expected better.

She wants things from you that you can't give. You're better off without her. Better off without all this.

His heart burned, calling him a liar.

Kairos came down the steps of the church, dressed in a tux. "Where is your bride? The wedding starts soon."

"I expect she'll be here."

"What have you done?"

"Nothing out of the ordinary."

"So," Kairos said, "something terrible."

Andres let out a derisive laugh. "It doesn't matter. She doesn't have anywhere else to go. She'll be here. She has no other choice."

"You are a fool," his brother said, the venom injected into his words a shock. "I have watched you squander yourself for years but I thought that you would learn. I thought you would not waste this."

"Waste what?" Andres asked, the words coming out in a roll of fog in the cold, snowy air. "My forced marriage?"

"She loves you," Kairos said, his voice low, vibrating with rage. "It is so clear to anyone who takes the time to look. Have you not?"

Andres's stomach tightened, regret lancing him like a sword. "I know." She would not love him now though. Not anymore. Of that he was certain.

"And still you betray her?" Kairos looked bleak. "You had the chance to have a woman look at you as she does...and you threw it away?"

"Attend to your own marriage and the lack of love in it and leave mine alone."

Kairos stepped forward, gripped the lapels on Andres's jacket and backed him against the church wall. "Do not speak of my marriage. You do not know what you're treading on."

"But you feel free to speak to me?"

"Yes. Because if I had a wife who looked at me the way she looks at you..."

"What? You'd do your very best to make sure she stopped?"

"Tabitha and I are not in love. We never have been."

"Perhaps you could have been."

"This," Kairos said, "is not about me. I am not the one who is supposed to be married in five minutes, has hundreds of guests in attendance and yet has no bride."

"She will be here."

"You had better hope so." Kairos turned and walked back into the church, closing the sanctuary doors behind him and leaving Andres outside in the snow.

But she didn't show. The snow began to fall harder, the temperature dropping as the day wore on. He imagined that people had left the church by now, spilling out the other entrance, leaving him alone here at the back, in the yard that bordered the cemetery and the woods.

He took a deep breath, but rather than making him feel refreshed, the frigid air let a burning, searing ache into his chest that he could scarcely breathe around. It was unendurable, unending.

And still, he stood and waited, even though he knew she would never appear. Even though he knew she wasn't going to come. He had done it. He had tested her feelings for him, and he had broken them.

Isn't it what you wanted?

He'd thought so. Had thought he would feel blessed relief at being released from her. From her expectations, if not her presence.

But he felt nothing like relief. He felt ruined.

Wasn't that the sick, sad thing about a man intent on self-destruction? He was bleeding out, and desperately wishing he could stop it. Even though he'd inflicted the wound. It was too late. All he could do was stand here, dealing with the consequences that he had earned. Consequences he had been aiming for. Consequences he didn't want.

You're in a hell of your own making.

Zara had told him that. Zara had been right.

But he was just so tired. So tired of wanting things and being denied. It was easier not to want them. Easier not to try. But Zara... Zara made him want. She made him think that it might be possible to have a life. To have love. A marriage.

There had been little windows of time where he'd been able to imagine forever with her. Where he had let himself dream of children, of her looking at him with love in her eyes every single day. But the more he wanted it, the more terrifying it became. The most beautiful dreams had a tendency to morph into the foulest of demons.

So he'd attempted to exorcise this demon before it had gotten him. But now he regretted it. And it was too late.

With that exorcism should have come freedom, but he felt that he'd only bound himself up tighter, pushed himself deeper into perdition.

The ache in his chest was overwhelming now. He couldn't speak past it, couldn't breathe past it. Before, he had tamped it down, medicated it with alcohol, with women. Surrounded himself with people so he could pretend that he wasn't desperately, terrifyingly alone.

So he could pretend he was somehow different than the boy locked away in his room.

For the first time he allowed himself to feel it. Really feel it. It was the monster under his bed, the one he had pretended wasn't there. He had buried it, drunk it away, ignored it, mocked it. But now it was going to consume him, and there was nothing he could do about it. Nothing he could do to stop it.

He realized for the first time he'd left part of himself locked away. So that he couldn't be hurt. Couldn't be rejected.

He loosened his tie, taking a step away from the church, toward the woods. He couldn't breathe. Maybe it was the tie. Maybe it was the collar on his shirt. He undid a button. Then the next. He still couldn't breathe. The constricting feeling was inside his throat, tightening, like a noose around his neck he couldn't reach or control.

He took another step away from the church, then another. And he refused to look back. He headed toward the trees, toward isolation. He felt driven to embrace it, driven to experience this moment of honesty. The first moment of honesty in his entire life.

He kept walking, the air around him darkening as the trees thickened.

He had always run into the crowd in moments like this. When the howling emptiness inside him became too much, he let it get swallowed up by people, things. But here he could do nothing but let it expand. Admit that Zara was right.

He'd been happy when his mother was gone because it meant no more trying. No more pain. No more failure in any way that mattered.

But Kairos had still demanded of him, and so he'd tried to rid himself of his brother too, though it hadn't worked. And all the while he'd told himself it was because he was every bit as evil as his mother had said.

Debauched. A mistake.

He was still just a boy locked in his room. Away from everything. No matter how many women he touched, no matter how many parties he went to… no one ever really reached him.

Until Zara.

And he'd betrayed her. Now he was alone again and there was no denying it. No covering it up.

Every year of isolation was catching up to him now, rolling over him in great, crashing waves. Years of it, threatening to suffocate him if he didn't relieve some of the pressure.

You could just go out into the woods and scream to make yourself feel better.

Another bit of wisdom from Zara. Feral wisdom. She was filled with it. She was nothing more than a tiny woman who had been raised just this side of civilized. And yet she had taught him everything.

Now he was in the exact place she had found herself years ago. Hurting. Lonely. Dying inside with no way to heal himself.

He had nothing to lose. No image to maintain. He had just been jilted in front of his entire country. He had been left by the only woman who had ever loved him. The only woman he had ever loved in return. And he was responsible. It was his fault. His fear had destroyed everything.

Because he had let it grow inside him, unidentified, ignored. He had pretended it wasn't there and like a malignant disease it had grown, thrived, as he had allowed it to. He had told himself his relief at his mother being gone made him terrible. Wrong.

He had simply been afraid. Admitting that was the hardest thing, admitting he was weak.

He'd imagined himself invulnerable. As long as he believed he feared nothing, as long as he believed he didn't care, it must be true. But it was a lie. It had always been a lie. It was his caring for his mother, her disdain for him that had made it a burden. If he'd never cared, it would not have felt so heavy.

He did care. And he had failed. Now it all rested on him.

He wanted to rail against it. He wanted to scream as Zara said she did when she came to the woods alone.

"Did you feel better?"

"Not really. But I could breathe."

The thought of doing that would have been impossible only a few hours ago. Because he was buried so deep inside himself, and screaming into the emptiness was letting it free. Letting that un-controlled boy who had cared, but had failed, out to try again. He had buried that boy. That boy who had been wrong, perpetually, to those who should have loved him simply for breathing.

He had grown into a man who had felt nothing for far too long. Who had been paralyzed in the end when he was offered the world.

A man who couldn't breathe.

He did his best to take a gasp of air, something, anything to fill his lungs. And then he shouted into the emptiness. Not words, just pain. Forcing it out of his body the best he could, clearing room so that he could breathe again. He wanted to be rid of the fear. Of everything he had allowed to stand in his way.

He had broken his own life. He could no longer blame anyone else. The one who held everyone at a distance. Who tried to prove to himself that the love he was offered was false. He had tested his mother. She had failed. She had failed and he had been glad because her love was so heavy.

He shouted again, the sound rough and raw in the silence. But when he was finished, he found that he could breathe again. Just for a moment it felt as if Zara was with him.

He wanted her to be. He realized that with blinding clarity as the sound of his voice faded into a distant echo. He wanted her to be with him so that neither of them would be alone again. But she could have anyone. Any future she wanted. She didn't have to make a life with him.

But he would ask. He would beg if he had to.

He had closed himself off to caring, to needing anyone else for fear that he might fail. He might very well fail at this. He didn't care. He wanted her, he wanted her forever, and that was worth the risk.

He would lay himself bare, open, without his heart and show it to her if need be.

But he would not let her walk away without a fight.

He was broken already. There was nothing to protect. And without her, he could never be put back together.

He did not know if he could be saved. But he knew one thing for certain: Her love was not heavy. It was light.

The only thing powerful enough to raise him back up from hell.

Everything inside Zara hurt. Everything on the outside of Zara hurt. She was pain wrapped in misery, rolled in regret and stuffed beneath the blanket she never wanted to emerge from. Of course, she couldn't take up permanent residence underneath a blanket in the guest room at Julia's. Convenient though it might be.

Today was her wedding day. She hadn't shown up. It was also her first real Christmas in years. She hadn't shown up for that either.

At least Christmas would keep coming. It always did. Every year, whether she was in a position to celebrate it or not.

Her wedding to Andres could only have happened today. The offer would never present itself again.

He betrayed you.

Yes, he had betrayed her.

She fought against the voice inside her that was shouting about the fact that he had betrayed her out of fear. That he had tried to push her away because things had gotten too intense between them. That he was doing to her the same thing he had done to Kairos. Testing her. Testing their love.

Well, even if it was true, she couldn't allow him to get away with it. He couldn't keep doing that to her. He was going to have to accept the fact that she loved him, and love her back, or they could have nothing.

She was tired of being alone, and she had realized that she could be alone even while sleeping in the same bed with him. If he kept her cut off emotionally, then they would never really be together. He had perfected the art of being alone in a crowded room, and she would not allow him to do the same thing with her.

She wanted to be different. She wanted to be loved. She wanted to feel close to him, not just skin to skin, but soul to soul. After a lifetime of being set apart, she didn't think it was too much to want. Too much to ask.

She would never be whole, not without him. But she would find something. She was determined. She'd found...a fullness in her life at the palace. During her time with him.

She would not allow him to drain it all away just because he was scared.

It was well past noon. She should be getting out of bed. Julia had gone away to visit family for the day, and had told Zara that she could have the run of the house. Her response was to get back into bed as soon as Julia had left.

On the upside, Zara felt that she might finally have a friend. There were positions open within the school system for helping children learn to read that didn't require special degrees. She could get on-the-job training. She was excited about that.

She'd been prepared to take her place as princess. To take her place at Andres's side. But without him, she was back to being where she was before. Just Zara.

No, not *just* Zara. She was Zara Stoica, and she was no longer in hiding. She would do what she could, all that she could, with what resources she could acquire. She would start at the school, but maybe someday there would be more.

Something she could do to benefit children like her. Children without mothers. Without a real home.

Thinking about children made her stomach cramp. It was still entirely possible that she could be having Andres's child. But of course, neither of them had talked about that when she stormed out last night. She hadn't even let herself think about it.

But, even if she was having his baby, they didn't need to be together. They would work something out.

She ignored the creeping feeling of dread that coated her skin in ice. The truth was, he was royalty. He was a very powerful man. If she was pregnant, he would probably take the baby from her.

Cross that bridge if you come to it.

It would be another week or so before she knew for sure. She would worry about it then. For now, she would just marinate in her pain.

She heard a very hard knock coming from the front of the house, and instinctively, she crawled in more tightly on herself, gripping the edges of the blanket and drawing her knees up to her chest.

The knock sounded again. She was not going to answer someone else's door.

She heard a voice, combined with the knock,

though she could not make out what the words were. The tone was loud, rough, very male. She found herself instinctively responding to it, uncurling and planting both sock clad feet on the floor.

She stood, and before she knew precisely what she was doing, she was walking out of the bedroom and toward the front door.

She knew who it was before she swung the door open and was met with a heartbreakingly familiar face.

Something inside her had known it was him. She was still connected to him, even though he had broken her. Even though she was angry. Even though she had left him at the altar. She knew that she always would be. No matter how far away she went, no matter how much independence she gained, she would never forget him. She would never truly leave him behind.

Part of her was horrified by that revelation. Part of her cherished it. Held it close. The same part of her that never wanted to let him go.

A foolish, *foolish* part of herself.

"What are you doing here?" she asked.

Before she could draw another breath, his arm was wrapped around her waist, and he had drawn her in close, his mouth crashing down on hers. He was kissing her, deep, hard with so much passion. He was putting all of himself into this, and she recognized the difference. Recognized last night for what it really was.

She pulled away from him. "You coward," she hissed. "How could you do that? To me? To us?"

"Because I *am* a coward," he ground out. "I am a fool. I am everything you accused me of being. And I am sorry. Zara." He cupped her cheek, brushing her hair back from her face. "I am so sorry."

"Being sorry doesn't take that kiss away. You touched her. You…you tried to hurt me. You *did* hurt me."

"I know," he said, his voice ragged. "I was so intent on destroying myself that I ignored the fact that I would be destroying you too. I had only just purposed to myself that I would tell you we would be partners. That there would be no feelings because I… I was afraid of wanting more. Then you said you loved me. I didn't believe you loved me enough, Zara. Not because I thought you were a liar, but because I have never believed anyone could love me. In some ways, I did not think it would truly devastate you. I thought… I thought it might set you free. But I will not pretend it was entirely for you, I will not even pretend that I thought of you even a little bit as I did it. I thought of me. Of all the pain I wanted to spare myself. Of the long years spent watching the light slowly dimming in your eyes as I forced you to fall out of love with me by virtue of the fact that I am unlovable."

"You are not."

"I am an adult. I understand that the rambunctiousness of a child should not have the power to drive a mother away, however purposeful it was in the end. I do. But what it doesn't change is the fact that... I wasn't sorry when she left. And that feeling... It was much easier to feel that it was my fault since I was relieved that acting out had pushed her away."

"It wasn't you. And she was... She made it so hard for you. You were a small boy. Of course it was hard to be anything but relieved."

"It made me want to test people," he said. "Kairos. You. To see if I could get rid of you as easily. My brother is stubborn. He would not allow it. You... I am so sorry. No one should have stayed after what I did. I do not deserve your loyalty."

She blinked rapidly. "Andres, I know what it is to lose people. I lost my family. It wasn't their choice, but I lost them all the same. I know what it's like to be afraid of suffering the same loss. It is why I... I was part of why no one ever got close to me in the clan. Because I could not bear to love another person again, out of fear. But you made me love you. Yesterday, I felt very much like I was living the same nightmare over again. But I realized that I was more than the things I had lost. Each person I have loved has added more to me. More to who I am. Including you. The loss of them, the loss of you, did not steal more than you gave. I am stronger for having loved you, and no matter what happens in the future, that can't be taken away. No matter what happens, it will always have been worth it."

"Even if you have to live the rest of your life with me?"

Her heart sped up, then stuttered to a halt, sinking down into her stomach. "I can't do that."

"Why not?"

"Because you wanting me isn't enough. You marrying me isn't enough. I need…"

"I love you," he said, the words coming out rushed, intense. "I love you, Zara. I have not said that to anyone in more years than I can count. I have not once admitted to myself that I desperately wanted someone to love me since my mother."

"Your mother…"

"I wanted her to love me, but it was always out of my reach. Better to have her gone. I told myself that. And I hated myself for it, but it was easier than admitting that…that I wanted very much to love someone and for them to love me back. That it destroyed me that I could not be what she wanted me to be. So it was easier to stop trying than to keep on and to fail. But I'm admitting it now. Because I'm more afraid of life without you than I am of making myself vulnerable. And that is a first."

"You love me," she repeated.

"Yes." He held her close, his eyes intent on hers. "I do. Almost from the first moment I met you. But I couldn't admit it. Do you think I routinely wash women's hair?"

"I imagine you probably don't."

"Never." He kissed her lips lightly. "And you imagine I am often captivated by small, burrowing creatures?"

"I am not a creature."

"If you are, you are a creature I love very much. You are unlike any woman, *anyone*, I have ever known. You wanted to know me. Not the man I pretended to be. You wouldn't allow me to be false with you. You have stripped my defenses, and that is why you are so dangerous to me. That is why I ran from you. Why I had to push you away. But as I stood there today, outside the church, alone, realizing you wouldn't be there, I wanted to take it all back. I've never wanted to take back one of my actions more in all of my life. Not what I did when my mother left, not what I did to my brother. Your loss. Yours. That was the one I could not survive."

"Andres." She said his name because she could think of nothing else to say. She leaned in and kissed him. In that kiss she poured every word she couldn't speak, every feeling she couldn't fully identify. Everything she wanted him to understand.

When they parted, they were both breathing heavily.

"Marry me," he said. "Not because you have to. Not because I have to. But because you want to. Because I would be lost without you."

"Yes," she said. "Yes."

"You are the best Christmas present I could ever have received. But I don't want to own you. I simply want to love you. So, as you were given to me, I give myself to you."

"I accept," she said. "And I couldn't ask for anything better. I love you, Andres. Now and forever. If I had every choice in the entire world open up to me, I would still choose you. Every time."

"And I you."

"I do hope, though, that this isn't the only Christmas present I get."

"Really? What else do you want?"

"I was thinking maybe a fruit basket."

He let his head fall back, a smile crossing his face, his laughter genuine and perfect and everything she had ever wanted. "That can be arranged. I think, also, that while it might be too late for us to get married with the entire country present, we can still have a Christmas wedding."

EPILOGUE

DARKNESS HAD FALLEN by the time Princess Zara, now of Petras—still not heiress to a throne, but feeling quite happy about the whims of one particular man—walked across the courtyard in her lace gown that glittered like the snow, toward her groom. Her dark hair was left loose and wild, swirling around her in the wind, gold paint dotting her forehead, and beneath her eyes. Only family and close friends of Andres and Kairos were there, but no one mattered to Zara or Andres but each other.

Soft light was filtering through the stained-glass window in the church, shining out onto the snow, casting colors around their feet. More flakes were falling softly around them, catching in Andres's dark hair, on his black suit jacket.

The air was thick with silence, but they weren't alone. They never would be again. Even when they were apart they would carry their love for each other in their hearts, and with that, emptiness could never have a chance to grow.

The priest began to speak their vows, his voice piercing the stillness. Zara closed her eyes and let the words wash over her.

"Do you, Princess Zara Stoica, give yourself to this man?"

She released her hold on one of his hands, taking a step forward and placing her palm against his cheek, making sure her eyes met his. "I do. I give myself to him, of my own free will. To love, from now to forever."

"And do you, Prince Andres Demetriou, give yourself to this woman?"

"I do," Andres said, his voice suspiciously rough, his dark eyes shining in the light. "I give myself to her, not out of a sense of honor, or duty to my brother or country, though I love them both. I give myself to her, to you, Zara, because I love you. Now and forever."

"Then I now pronounce you husband and wife."

Andres didn't wait for permission to gather her in his arms and kiss her. He had never been very good at waiting for permission, but Zara considered it one of his charms.

One of his many charms.

When they parted, she smiled. "When I was a child I lost my home. I lost my family. And today, you have given me both. You are my home. You are my family."

He closed his eyes, resting his forehead against hers. "And you are mine. You are mine."

* * * * *

LARGER-PRINT BOOKS!

GET 2 FREE LARGER-PRINT NOVELS PLUS
2 FREE GIFTS!

HARLEQUIN®

Romance

From the Heart, For the Heart

READERSERVICE.COM

Manage your account online!

- Review your order history
- Manage your payments

YATES Maisey (ROMANCE)
Yates, Maisey
A Christmas vow of seduction

- Discover new series available to you, and read excerpts from any series.
- Respond to mailings and special monthly offers.
- Connect with favorite authors at the blog.
- Browse the Bonus Bucks catalog and online-only exculsives.
- Share your feedback.

Visit us at:

ReaderService.com